# MIND SHIFT

Vol. 5 of the
Three Worlds Saga

Carol A. Strickland

**Other books by Carol A. Strickland**
*Touch of Danger* – vol. 1 of the Three Worlds Saga
*Lost in the Stars* – vol. 2 of the Three Worlds Saga
*Worlds Apart* – vol. 4 of the Three Worlds Saga
*Mind Shift* – vol. 5 of the Three Worlds Saga
*Secrets of the Worlds* – vol. 6 of the Three Worlds Saga
*Applesauce and Moonbeams* – wacky soft sci fi
*Nothing Personal* – ditto but wackier
*Burgundy and Lies* – sweet historical romance
*Star-Spangled Panties* – the full nonfiction dish on Wonder Woman!

# 1

"**P**oisoned?!"

Carolina Starhart stared at the three Affiliated Systems Mega-Legionnaires who faced her, looking remarkably blasé about their findings at the food-laden break table set up in the back of the hotel's lecture hall. In a little while she was supposed to be conducting an important workshop here on the alien world of Deseed. They awaited her response.

How could they be so calm when she boiled with frustration at the situation? Bad enough that she'd hardly been able to sleep last night in fear of teaching the classes, but–

Poison! How *dare* anyone try to–

After all she'd been through these past three weeks. Damn whoever did this anyway! She'd been run through the universe's wringer, then "treated" to tests that would have left anyone else twitching in a corner. Maybe not these guys, though. They were mega-heroes, pros at facing Armageddon.

Minzier here was a hulking blue Legionnaire whose left eyebrow merely twitched at her as he relayed the news. She knew Minzier only because he'd escorted her and her husband Londo to prison from her trial a couple weeks ago and Lon had spoken with him. He was a member of Lina's other husband Jae's Alpha Team and a friend of Lon, while Chimrin, this lavender-skinned woman with wary features and an equally wary mind, had been Legion Commander when Lon and Jae were in their early teens and still new to the Legion.

The third person she didn't know, other than that he was yet another Mega-Legionnaire, clad in the same general type of clingy costume the others wore, and just as unfazed as the other two. Powers up the wazoo and used to all hell breaking loose.

But Lina wasn't. After living through the recent terrors, she deserved a rest from the wrath of the chaos gods.

Oh, she hoped there weren't really chaos gods.

Then she realized what the three were telling her.

*Someone* had *poisoned* the food this other-planetary hotel had set out for the good people who were about to attend her seminar.

The worlds of both the Affiliated Systems and unaffiliated planets wanted to learn how to get rid of Mind Control once and for all. She could teach them. Meanwhile the nearby Yanist-Glory Empire was keen to extend its borders, and Mind Control was its favorite tool to accomplish that. Through it, innocents could be turned into helpless puppets, unable to fight would-be oppressors.

But as she expanded her psychic healing side business back on Earth, Lina had developed the trick of releasing such Control. Until she'd traveled off-world with Londo and then with Jae, she'd never realized that Mind Control could be such a problem. Now the three of them had organized a tour of several planets during which she'd teach hundreds of people the trick. They'd make videos so others could learn as well, expanding her teachings across the worlds.

Now the ugliness she had been warned to expect had begun so suddenly. Lina swallowed hard. So someone thought they'd just kill off everyone who learned how to counter them, tra-la.

Lina had been frightened down to her very cells at too many points these past weeks, but now she discovered she was still uncalloused enough that fear could slash its way through her. Emperor Yanist-Glory, famous for his Mind Control tactics, had cruelly treated Londo when he was a child, kidnapping him and experimenting on him until he gained powers. Lon and his Mega-Legion troops had just waged a war here on Deseed to prevent the emperor from taking over. So many had been Mind Controlled. They were waiting for someone to free them.

But it wasn't only the emperor's forces. Stoan Kinrol, the current Legion commander, had been enslaved and then Controlled by otherwise ordinary people when he was a young man. He'd been used for assassination so that his owners could profit. Mind Control was a tricky business, but those without ethics could accomplish it with the high tech available Out Here in interstellar space.

Poison. To stop her and her students. Lina felt the blood begin to drain from her head. The room started to spin, just a trifle, before she set her jaw.

She was *not* going to faint in front of Legionnaires!

Four days ago, she'd managed to faint in front of most of the cameras of Earth. In retrospect: mortifying! No, there would be no fainting now.

Especially since – wonder of wonders – the Legionnaires were looking to *her* to tell them what to do next. This was her project, not theirs. Chimrin squinted at her. Without reading her mind – or vice versa – Lina knew Chim was urging her on to her new position as Speaker for the Three Worlds.

Weeks ago, the entities that embodied the worlds of Earth, Aldierra, Sarastor – and Jae's destroyed home of Feith, observing in the background – had appointed Lon, Jae and herself as their Chosen. Their mission was to improve those three worlds whose humans were traveling the wrong path.

"How'd this happen?" Lina asked the three. "I mean, the Legion was supposed to provide security for all this. Somebody miss a memo?"

"Things can slip through," Chim told her in clipped syllables. "This is why you have to keep your guard up all the time, from all directions."

Chim had been hounding the three of them: Lon, herself, and Jae, to take specialized self-defense classes and more since their new relationship had changed everything. Now Londo, the mighty Valiant, was vulnerable whenever she or Jae touched him. As a norm leading an everyday life, Lina had never needed to learn self-defense. If the three of them were to function as a team or just as a couple, or triple, they'd have to relearn how to act around each other, especially if they were under attack.

And now here was something else to bolster that idea. Gah. Lina wasn't ready for this. But she had to be. So much depended upon her.

The third guy started to gather up the food in bags. "How're the drinks?" Lina asked.

"Poisoned." As if *of course*.

"Well. I can't have my students going hungry. It'll distract them. Can the hotel–"

"We're interrogating the staff and delivery personnel," Minzier reported. "By the second session we might have some other source available. Maybe. You really think you need to feed them?"

"The class is going to take seven or eight hours. I need these students paying attention to what they need to learn, not thinking about their empty stomachs."

All righty then. Lina brushed off the bottom of her tee shirt just to get rid of nervous energy. "I'll hit Earth for food." Then she scratched the back of her head. "Although I don't have any money left."

"Use my card. *La voici.*"

The welcome voice came from behind, and as her heart leaped inside her she turned to the reassuring sight of her new husbands, Londo and Jae, ambling into the room. They were both in their costumes; Londo's Valiant suit so familiar to her from years of appearances on the Terran news, and Jae's Neutrino uniform becoming more so as she learned about him and his own interplanetary exploits.

Londo was a prince of a man, a Hercules with dark hair, light brown skin, and that black outfit that showed off his form so well. He strode in as if he owned the room, maybe the planet as well. He was a force of nature.

Jae's skin was a shade darker than Lon's, but he had a mass of shoulder-length blond hair that looked entirely natural on him because it was. The length likely drove Legion Protocol nuts, but Jae was the Last Feithi, and even the Legion's sacred Rules didn't mess with that. He was taller than tall Londo, leaner than him, and his stride was liquid.

"Someone's poisoned–" Lina pointed at the emptying table and the bags. Minzier now held the four urns containing drinks in his broad arms. Lina tried not to laugh from hysteria. They'd chosen to furnish fresh food and drinks buffet-style to neutralize the possibility of hacked replicators. So much for that idea.

"We heard," Jae said.

"Kuttr's heading the interrogations," Lon told her. "It won't take long to see how they accomplished this. And who they take their orders from."

Chim said, "I'd better join him." She was a telepath, expertly trained and skilled in the arts a megapara hero needed to know to accomplish their job. She left with the others.

Only the Starharts were left. Jae couldn't officially add the surname to his, not until Londo agreed to release the secrecy of the Feithi Triune marriage they'd entered into. But he was her husband now. It worried Lina that she didn't have as deep a connection with him as she did with Lon, but she hadn't known Jae as long as she'd known Lon. Why, there were at least two days' difference. Hm, she hadn't quite realized until now just how busy those two days had been. Oh well, they would have time to even things out since they were marriage-vowed to longer than forever.

But for now, they were pressed for time.

Lina held out her hand expectantly for Lon's card.

"We'll all go," he told her, his no-nonsense tone in full employ. The French-Canadian accent made it more riveting. "*Fais attention.* Remember."

"Security. Your safety." Jae finished for him.

Never argue with stone walls. With a sigh of surrender Lina ported the three of them. After two minutes of dark void, they stood on Earth. Lina was an interstellar teleporter. The only reason her ports weren't instantaneous was that she needed time to filter out contagions and adjust for pressure and electrical differentials from world to world.

Instead of taking them to Starhaven, their new Wyoming home (under much construction), she brought them to her friend Dodger's bakery in Eno Valley, North Carolina.

It was late morning and only one clerk was behind the glass cases, bending over to pick something off the checkerboard floor. She rose, gave a squeak at being surprised by unannounced customers, and then let out a shriek.

Dodger called out from the back even as they could hear his pounding feet. "What? Nicole, are you–"

"Vuh… Vuhh!" Nicole attempted to speak while her jaw had dropped. "Valiant!" She finally managed, pointing at Londo, clad in his worlds-famous outfit of black pants, boots, and hunter's vest.

Jae chuckled and put his hand on Lon's shoulder, which drew the woman's attention. Her mouth remained open, but her eyes widened even further as she took him in as well, with his blue costume and billowing white cape. "Ohh!"

Lina tried not to laugh. That had pretty much been her own reaction when meeting them the first time, though for her it had been on an individual basis.

Dodger, in white apron and both hair and beard nets, stood in the doorway to the kitchen, unable to move. Syllables came from his mouth that had no meaning to anyone but him.

"Dodger!" Lina said, sharp enough to rouse him but not too sharply, she hoped. "We need to buy you out. Well, pretty much."

He blinked a few times before he noticed she stood there. "Lina? Lina! Are you okay? I saw you on TV. You looked–"

"I'm okay now. They have great doctors Out There," she assured him as he rushed to the counter.

"Out There?"

Lina pointed up, into the far heavens. "Way Out There. Londo, this is Dodger Snipes, baker supreme. Dodger, Londo Starhart." They nodded to each other, one rather dazedly.

"Taller," Dodger managed to say. "You're taller than you look on TV. And… really tall." His gaze slid to Jae, who stood a good four inches above Londo.

Yep, Lina knew her guys were spectacular. "This is Jae… Rallene, also known Out There as Neutrino." She repeated the introductions for Nicole, who could only gaze at Jae's perfect face in ecstasy. Jae managed to do all the handshaking with his right hand while scratching his neck with his left.

Lina figured they both probably ran into this kind of thing all the time. "I'd love to chat, but some bad guys Out There have sabotaged a workshop I'm giving."

Dodger was about to say something but stopped to blink. He seemed to be trying to keep up with all the Out There and Valiant and people in costume and Lina being in the headlines these past few days. "Sabotaged?"

"Our hotel arranged snacks and drinks, and it all came in poisoned."

"Poisoned?" Nicole squeaked.

Lina nodded. "That's what I said. So we need a butt-load of snacks from you to feed everyone. Some kind of lunches, too. It's a long seminar with a pretty big crowd scheduled. I'm going to send Lon off to get some healthy stuff. Grocery's next door, Lon."

He looked through the wall. "I see it. Healthy, you say?" He rubbed at his left ear.

"Don't pick at that," Jae muttered. Lon shrugged, lowered his hand from his new earring, and returned his gaze to the group,

"Fruit and party trays of chopped veggies to counter this. Sandwiches. Soups. I don't think the silverware was affected, or napkins. Hand wipes? Don't know about glasses."

Lon checked a padd he'd produced from his vest. "We're good on those."

Lina nodded. "I want to say there are a hundred and fifty participants, something like that. Do you think they'll have things figured out for the second seminar?"

Jae was checking over Lon's shoulder at the padd's readout. "We are the Legion. Just worry about the first class, Lie. I'll make sure we're ready for the next one, no matter what develops."

"Oh good." Lina closed her eyes for a moment in relief but had to open them again. No time, no time.

The bakery's displays were filled with doughnuts, cookies, cake slices, and yum. "We need some tea too, Dodger. You got any made up?"

He draped one arm over his display case, trying to look cool when Lina thought he might need it to support his wobbly legs. "That's one thing I can certainly supply," he told her. "Last night our ice machine gave out, right out of the blue. I've been trying to fix it. It won't freeze. We haven't sold a drop of tea yet, not without any ice in house. How many gallons do you need?"

Jae nodded at him. "We should have anticipated something like that," he confided. "*Someone* was expecting us to need drinks. Sorry about the trouble."

He acknowledged Dodger's puzzled expression with a slight grimace and Lina said, "Thank you, Earth," as she looked at the floor. The world entities they worked with sometimes arranged odd help for them.

Jae scratched his chin. "I'll see about your… ice machine? It freezes water? I can take care of that at least temporarily."

"Jae can… change things," Lina tried to explain.

"I alter the structure of the universe," Jae clarified. "Matter and energy. Liquid water to ice, in this case. It comes in handy."

"I… bet it does," Dodger managed. He cocked his head from side to side. "Are you Irish?"

That garnered him a wrinkled nose. "Londo gave me English lesson… tapes. Apparently they contained an accent."

"Ah."

"In the meantime, we'll take the tea." Jae checked with Lina. "It's acceptable?"

She gave him a smile. "Dodger makes great tea."

Jae turned to Londo. "Lina is picky about her tea."

Lon was busy scribbling on his padd. "So I'm learning. I can handle the ice if you want."

"No, I've got it," Jae assured him.

Lina told Dodger, "Jae makes great ice, I bet. Lon? The card?"

Lon didn't offer it. "I'll need it for more than just next door. There're a few fast-food places down the road that have lunch salads made up already. I'll clean them out, see how much we can get out of that." He pointed at something far beyond the parking lot. "A catering place. Looks like they're gearing up for a large party. I'll make it worth their while to sell us some of that food." Then he grimaced. "What to carry it all in?"

Dodger dared to speak up. "I h-have some r-racks." He waved to the back of his store. "Will those do?"

Lon checked with his paravision and gave him a grin, which Dodger was delighted to return. "Perfect. It should take five, six trips. You up for that, Lina?"

"No sweat. Steal some shopping carts while you're next door. That'll cut down on the trips."

"We'll return them before class begins. Let's give these folks an introduction to Terran cuisine." Then the mightiest megahero in the galactic sector set off to buy groceries.

2

Lina peeked at the crowd from behind the stage's screens. It was by far the largest class she'd ever taught, and the most important. One hundred and forty people from different worlds sat expectantly in the room's chairs, some of them finishing a danish or carrot stick, all carefully wrapped so as not to provide the skin-to-food contact that people Out Here found distasteful.

A hundred and forty!

She wasn't good with crowds. Back on Earth before she'd become a teleporter, her few, fill-in psychic classes for her friend and mentor Sue Taylor had consisted of a maximum of fifteen people.

She swallowed. She'd gotten through those classes. She could do this.

Lord, everyone was a stranger.

No, she couldn't do this.

She *had* to. Picture the people, the worlds to be saved.

Six who were not strangers were her friends from the Raleigh-Durham area, people who had taken Sue's classes in a wide spectrum of New Age arts: tarot, astrology, channeling, mediumship, psychic healing, and such alongside Lina a few years ago and stuck together afterward as they all learned more on their own. Lina had specialized in healing, psychic readings, and communicating with her angel guides. For this event their teacher herself was attending, eager to help and learn. They would catch on to Lina's techniques quick enough and be able to assist her as the class progressed. All had been given floating marble translators, so language was no problem.

David, of course, had ignored suggestions about people covering up as much skin as possible. AffSys types were allergic to seeing arms and legs and the bottoms of necks, it seemed. Instead many liked to wear pleated parachutes. Lina was always getting in trouble over that. The Legion issued demerits to spouses.

But here non-Legion-related David would get away with it. He wore a short-sleeved rock band tee with jeans; just had to break the rules. Cantrell's suit fully covered him in a colorful kente print. He said he wanted to represent Earth and not just the US. Good point.

The women of the group wore long-sleeved shirts over jeans and slacks, except for Elena, who came in a pretty dress, with dark tights underneath. Sue's jewel-toned sequined show jackets had been left behind, thank goodness. Instead she wore her familiar plum-colored "I'm leading a serious workshop" suit, even though she wasn't for this one, but still made Lina feel at home here on this alien world.

Seven semi-recognized faces were from Tishan, the secretive world of telepaths. The Tishana Legionnaire Chimrin Dinar had arranged for them to learn the process and assist as long as Tishana authorities promised not to interfere with distribution of the classes' videos. All the Tishana were suited up in proper, sedate parachute suits. Chim herself was in the audience here, dressed in more spandex-y civilian clothing but still looking alert and Legionnaire-ish. She'd learned the basics by helping Lina four days ago and could help now while the assistants were still on a learning curve. By the time this session was over she'd be completely trained, as would be the assistants.

Unobtrusive cameras floated here and there around the room to record. At least they were video and not still cameras. Lina was terrified of still cameras pointed at her. Darn Dad anyway. On the rare occasions that his camera had ever aimed her way, he spent the time criticizing her, reiterating that her burdensome existence was a shame to all. In her mind, still photos existed to focus upon her shortcomings.

Some of the class participants were talking with their seatmates in an animated way. Their facial expressions were not happy ones. They gestured at the space in front of their seated selves, some of them forming a frame with their hands and then making puzzled movements.

Her fault. She didn't want the seats to have individual info screens. As it was, she'd insisted that everyone leave their communication devices outside the lecture hall. Students shouldn't zone out of the workshop by cruising the interstellar Internets for more information… or porn. They needed to pay attention to the big front screen.

This of course didn't apply to the Mega-Legionnaires, who were required to wear their Legion Array at all times unless they were sleeping. The Array held all kinds of communication channels for them, protective doodads she had yet to fully discover, as well as a device that allowed them to fly. Lon had snuck part of an Array onto her once, a highly illegal move, and she had floated around for a few minutes. It was scary but wonderful. The lesson came in helpful once she realized that one of her new powers was that of levitation.

The Legion needed its communications. Since the Legion was supplying immediate security for the Tour, Lina agreed to that exception.

"Are we good?" she whispered to Dr. Wilder Mem-Bazer, the middle-aged, azure-skinned genius with five minds.

He was wearing a bulky civilian outfit consisting of layers of light material and odd pleats, a typical parachute suit, ugh. But who was she to turn up her nose at Proper Fashion? Still, she preferred Wiley's usual lab coat. His hair was a natural shade of purple, short but pleasantly non-buzzed, unlike most AffSys hairstyles. It often stuck out where he rubbed his head while thinking his deep thoughts. She resisted the impulse to cower behind him.

His eyes studied different, invisible screens in front of him, tracking separately. For Wiley, of course, any kind of information-gathering system was essential. "Recording commencing. Have you journaled?"

"I thought I'd begin that after this session. Up until now I didn't have anything much to say, did I?"

That elicited a dissenting grunt from Wiley. He had instructed the three of them that they had a duty to history to record this journey that the Three Worlds had commanded of them. His logs of the Three Worlds Investiture included readings of massive psychic phenomena – ghosts and sentient planetary entities – that had awed and mystified even Tishana experts.

Wiley had heard and chronicled Aldierra's message of doom to the Aldierrans. Then Lina had de-Controlled several Legionnaires, explaining to him and his cameras how she was doing it. She and his two Legion teammates stood at the crux of a turning point for the galactic sector. What would a sector without Mind Control look like? Mind #2 in Wiley's head gleefully churned away at the hypotheses. Could they really accomplish this?

"Include information that is previous to this. The Investiture. The trial. Your biography. It's all important to history."

To that Lina gave her own grunt. History. Well, she supposed it might be at that. Really? Really. "I made sure my hair was braided tight," she said. "Are you getting a good picture?"

"What, from your earring?" Wiley had issued special impervion earring posts to them. While Jae had always worn a single earring and Lina, two, it had taken the both of them to figure out how to pierce Londo's left ear. Like Jae's, the earring sat halfway up the outer ear and not in the lobe: the Fethi way, even if Lon didn't have

Jae's pointed ears. They were fairly certain the piercing would hold, but with an invulnerable person the cells could heal over if they got a mind to. They'd keep an eye on how things went. The tiny posts held all kinds of audio/visual equipment.

"I told you," Wiley said, "the system will have no problem with seeing around your hair. Or corners."

"Just–"

"No sex," he assured her. "The system has instructions to stop recording at the first hint of it."

Lina wasn't sure she could trust Wiley about that, but he was a close friend of her husbands, and already one to her.

She blew out a shaky breath. One hundred and forty.

Like it or not, it was showtime. "You should join the audience," she said as she adjusted her outfit. Jae had chosen a comfortable Feithi fashion design for her from the puters, complete with the colorful ribbons and ties that had been in vogue at the time of his planet's demise, and Lon had adapted it so it looked more "woo-woo," as he put it. Lon had come a long way in accepting psychic and metaphysical ideas, but that didn't mean he'd stopped making fun of them.

Her friend Dinah Stewart had exclaimed, "It's so Olivia Newton-John!" when she'd shown up this morning. Well, Lina decided she liked her silky disco skater jumpsuit dress. It proclaimed "New Age guru" in an understated way. Unlike so many other outfits she'd been forced to put on lately, this not only allowed her to wear underwear, but also covered her up. Legion Protocol would approve. Pretty much. She had variants standing by for different classes, some more dress and some more jumpsuit, but all fairly white. Despite the poor contrast between the material and her pale skin, she'd need that color to help with psychic energy protection as the lectures progressed.

Beneath the suit, taped securely to her chest for safekeeping, lay the ruby amulet of a rogue Galactic Guard. She could sense its relief to be away from Granger and under her protection. She wasn't going to let it fall into the wrong hands again!

She'd accomplished the impossible then. But now…

Jae and Londo had had their own way of trying to get her to relax last night. She didn't even try to hide her smile as she remembered. Individually they were dynamite, but oh my, they worked so well as a team.

And it had worked last night. She'd gotten a little sleep afterward. But now…

She. Could. Do. *This.*

In her mind she pictured herself jumping from one cliff to another. She'd metaphorically, and sometimes not so metaphorically, done that a few times these past weeks.

Take a step in the right direction. Don't turn back. No, there was no possibility of turning back. The only way was forward.

Wiley had taken his seat. *Jump.* Lina emerged from the holographic curtain. The parachuted audience quieted instantly, something she wasn't used to. People Out Here were trained to obey society's rules.

"G-good morning. My… My name is Carolina Starhart. Call me Lina. I am the Speaker for the Three Worlds, which are Sarastor, Earth and Aldierra. Welcome to the first session in the Three Worlds Mind Control Tour. In the next few hours, we're going to show you how to eliminate the threat of Mind Control from your worlds. You'll also receive a *raasch* of this class that you can take home with you and show your people."

Lina tried not to entertain ideas of what these strangers thought about her, someone they up to now had heard of only as Valiant's bride. She was some no-name Terran, so short (though she'd always been pointed out as "that tall girl" back before she'd left Earth), so pale in a sector where people seemed to run to mid-tones, though they spread them over the rainbow. Skin colors settled primarily in the peachish-tan and blue ranges, though this crowd contained a couple of purples and one bright green man.

At least she had her hair firmly braided at the back of her head so they couldn't stare at that. Most of these people held to two inches or less, if not zero, hair. Head hair wasn't politically correct Out Here, and the mop of curling auburn that both Londo and Jae admired so much reached three-quarters of the way to Lina's waist unless she had it braided or pinned up. One of Jae's friends had complained that she had enough hair for a small army. That young woman had been bald except for three scraggly patches of prickle. She'd also had a tattooed tongue.

Focus on one section of attendees at a time, maybe ten. Not a hundred and forty. Ten she could handle. Make it eight.

Lina gave a quick outline of how the session would progress with a warning that this might go long, as everyone, including the assistants, was being trained. She reminded them that very serious guards stood beyond each exit, and outside breaks would not be allowed unless there were an emergency. The few Legionnaires they might spot inside the auditorium were there to learn, though they could be summoned for security as well.

Lina smiled and smiled, trying to set the crowd at ease. Surely they'd heard the rumors that she was a Terran barbarian witch doctor. Lon had reminded her to smile and relax. Jae said she had a lovely smile. She smiled just thinking of them but then reluctantly brought her mind back on topic. This was important; *don't mess it up.*

She told her audience that all sentients should be free to be whoever they needed to be, and that included slaves. "It should be considered absolutely immoral to own or impede another's thoughts, will, or body," she told them. To hell with Legion rules about conforming to the Affiliated Systems' code of laws, which condoned slavery on some worlds where the practice had been grandfathered in. They'd made it clear to that awful Commander Stoan Kinrol, aka Magnos, that this tour was a Three Worlds production, and not one of his Mega-Legion.

Though they welcomed the Legion's security.

Her notepadd triggered the room's audiovisual systems to show a 3-D representation of the human body and its aura overlaid with the seven major chakras, or energy centers. Mind Control, she told them, happened when a person threw harpoon-like intention "hooks" from their chakras into multiple chakras of another person, taking over their will.

She explained what she'd seen through the years, knowledge that had been expanded by experts Out Here: that a telepath who had been artificially boosted in power could Control, as well as a natural psychic who'd had their brain's ethics centers removed. Natural telepaths and un-eviscerated psychics could not usually accomplish Mind Control. Egotism of such magnitude partnered with low frequencies of spirit, which telepaths and psychics operated above. Even an average human with ordinary, natural psychic ability usually operated on frequencies higher than those of Mind Control, though now and then Hooks Happened.

Humans were emotional creatures. Strong emotions, either spur-of-the-moment or from a long grudge or mental imbalance, could spawn hooks. The worst of these were unconsciously created and sometimes maintained, but Mind Control with capital letters required skill and conscious intent to construct absolute hold.

Lina twitched her fingers and rolled her left wrist in the way Londo had shown her, signaling the program to change to a diagrammed animation of what hooks were. She winced when the stick figure on screen jerked at a hook's penetration into his throat chakra, and then trembled like Wile E. Coyote on earthquake pills as more hooks hit more chakras, beginning with the solar plexus one, the seat of personal power. Jae and Lon had had too much fun making the cartoon, egging on each other for more gruesomeness.

But each and every person here paid rapt attention to it.

That done, she split the workshop into smaller groups, thank goodness, each led by an assistant who'd received the briefest of briefings before beginning. The amphitheater's floors leveled off in spots so each group would have their own area to practice. From the stage she directed them all: how to center themselves and feel their own chakras, then line them up and clear themselves of excess negativity.

She taught them how to protect themselves with universal white light, and how to receive spiritual help if they got in trouble. She took them through exercises in which they experimented with their own auras, ones in which they used crayons to draw others' auras and compared how well they matched within their own groups.

Everyone paired up and felt each other's energy, then did a chakra balance on each other, which allowed them to feel and work with chakras, as well as clean them much more from how they'd entered the room. As she circulated through the groups to supervise, Lina noticed the Tishana being surprised by the effects.

She paused and turned to Wiley. He had been following her, then roaming around the groups, peering at everyone, then following her again. "You come here on vacation?" she asked the non-participant. "You're spooking them. And me. Stop it."

"I'm observing this session for Legion purposes," he replied. His baggy parachute jumpsuit was patterned in a bold geometric design but at least in sedate colors. A heavy tool belt hung from his waist, although Lina didn't think that handyman tools were in it. Rather, the highest-tech toys and tricorders probably lurked there, linked in some fashion through all those rings he wore and the multiple sensory inputs he'd had installed in himself to service his five minds.

"I've got extra sensors set up to record variations in the auras. I didn't know that ordinary people had hooks in them normally, but look here. Those aren't Mind Control, are they?" He showed her screens with auric scans of several participants. A few quill-like structures on each stood out of the smoother boundaries of each auric level.

Lina shook her head. "We'll get to that in the next part." It had been she who had shown him how the aura operated. One of his minds – or maybe more – had figured out how to get a bit of the aura work on tape. Sooner or later, she'd learn the science behind it. But not now.

"Aren't you a Team Leader?" Lina teased. "Doesn't that require you to take the course? I don't give slackers a passing grade."

"I'm not a Team Leader, but I'm at Team Leader level," he replied with a small smile. "I'll officially take the course toward the end of the tour. I want to see how what you teach changes between now and then. It invariably will. You'll add some items and modify techniques. I want to see as well if the Tishana are going to have any input by the end of this."

Everyone took a long break and then resumed to learn how to feel for hooks. They worked on each other in pairs or triples, removing the negative hooks that they already had, for almost everyone had some kind. As they removed them, they learned how to differentiate between benign hooks, usually formed through close relationships, and hooks that could be harmful. They also learned how to pull in more light, to wipe away clouding fields that might hide hooks, and how to hum or sing to raise or lower vibration.

Many of the students balked at the idea of humming – Out Here music was a sign of barbarism – but when they saw the Tishana doing it (per Chim's unquestioned orders), showing the students that it wasn't fatal, everyone tried it and found that it worked well.

The Tishana clearly weren't used to such informal instruction but they had a healthy respect for the Legion's ex-Commander, a force to be reckoned with.

After another break involving a small meal, and a warning for telepaths present with a reminder that barf bags had been issued to every participant, the Legionnaires in the room turned on mental dampers that Wiley had recently invented. Guards pulled shackled "zombies," as the Mind Controlled were called, into the room. Here on Deseed there were thousands of them. They were pawns of last week's war that the Legion had instigated. This was the perfect world to find people to practice on.

The victims blinked as they entered and found themselves no longer linked to a controller. Though they'd been protected in their holding camps by dampers, the transportation to this venue had allowed Control to reinstate itself. One zombie was issued for each student, and within ninety minutes they all had their hooks removed.

The dampers switched off; the victims were unfazed and unControlled. Now Lina taught them how to call upon the white light to keep themselves free from future Mind Control. Three of the Tishana did deep telepathic scans of the former zombies, and then gathered to formulate a report to their home world.

One hundred and forty ex-Mind Controlled people left the auditorium to enjoy a world they were no longer cut off from. They could safely return to their homes and families. When Lina dismissed them, the audience gave her a standing ovation. She blushed and motioned to her assistants, Terran and Tishana alike, to receive the applause as well.

Lina looked forward to a very late lunch, hold the poison.

CHAPTER

3

Londo blinked at the sudden light as he and Jae appeared from the teleport onto the surface of Aldierra. He examined the environs, turning his head from side to side as he looked beyond surfaces with his paravision. Things didn't seem improved from the first and only time he'd been here, when an attempted revolt had broken out in government headquarters.

Before her first class, Lina had placed them where Jae had directed: in front of a towering concrete-like building. This was where the planet's governing councils controlled the world. It utilized basic trussed tubes but hardly tried exploring any creative design that structure allowed. There was no grace to it. Despite its height it felt squat and uninspiring. Londo's college architecture instructors would have had a fit seeing it.

The tips of the building's plaza neighbors tried to exploit the dull sunlight so they could shine, while the streets below were littered with waste of both the everyday living and human varieties. A man squatted in a gutter just down the block from this elite location, doing his business there as other men passed, oblivious.

There were no women in sight.

But there were many, many men, shouldering their way through the sprawling city on wide walkways. Their clothing was loose but trouser-like. Shirts came in short sleeves as well as long, and the day must have been cool, for some wore a kind of walking cape or shawl draped over themselves.

They wore masks that covered their noses and mouths, and goggles over their eyes. Lon noted that there were a few in the multitude, those huddled against walls or seated in alleys, who did not wear such protection. They suffered spells of wracking coughs, but so did some of the masked ones.

No windows penetrated the lower three stories of any building in sight. The loud, large automated vehicles that made up most of the traffic did not have windows. Inside them, Lon could see the packed cars provided individual computer screens for their passengers. Communications and entertainment made up most of the content. Lon peered closer to note the heavy shielding on each vehicle, much more than enough to handle speed mishaps. These cars were armored against violence. So were the flying vehicles that sometimes dipped alarmingly below what he considered safe levels.

An industrial smog hazed the sky to a grayish purple. Lon glanced to his side to make sure Jae had his uniform's air filter activated. With his own invulnerability, the harsh conditions wouldn't bother him, but Jae did not have that protection other than what his uniform – and his powers – provided. Even without normal clouds, a fine drizzle of dust and particles drifted down. The stench of burn surrounded them: wood, plastics, sugar, unknown chemicals.

"Good god, where do we begin?" Londo muttered even as he spotted a fight breaking out a mile away: two middle-aged men ambushed by a crowd of younger ones, with a few older ones mixed in. He crouched to take off in flight to break it up, but Jae touched his shoulder.

"We only handle the big concepts," Jae told him. "We have an entire planet to save."

"But…" It went against everything Londo believed. "Look, there's – there's a riot over there. And two more a few miles from here." He pointed at locations Jae wouldn't be able to see. "People are being hurt. Killed. I've got to go. I am this world's protector," he told Jae, but Jae held him back.

"You'll protect it best by handling the big problems. We'll get to the small stuff eventually – if we come through the Deadline."

The sentient planetary entity that was Aldierra had given her people that deadline and warning: *improve or die.* Lina had been the one to deliver the channeled message to every individual native of the world.

Now the Aldierran government was scrambling to attend to the problem. The three Starharts decided to use the week they'd been told would be all that the Aldierrans needed to formulate strategy and organize new agencies for action, to produce the Mind Control Tour. Today's visit was to check in to see what the government was planning. The Starharts would set up systems and coordinate as they could, but this was something the people of the world had to do themselves.

After the Tour they'd attend to Aldierra full-time. An itch ran down Lon's invulnerable spine that this might not be a simple overseeing, advising, and coordination job.

"Aldierra will not die on our watch," his telepathic husband vowed next to him. Jae's legendary world of Feith had been destroyed by the greed and jealousy of outsiders when he'd been a child. Jae was the lone survivor, the Last Feithi.

Deadline: Nine months away, more or less. No, don't say less. It was actually a tiny amount more time before this world decided whether to kill every native human on it or not.

From the filth, the anger, and the hopelessness Londo saw at every turn, it looked like they'd need every second of that.

Lon spotted more fights. An attack of some kind. A series of small riots – some not so small – taking place across the continent.

People getting hurt. His gut ached to see it. His fists curled in frustration.

But Jae was Team Leader on these first trips to Aldierra. During its attempted invasion of Sarastor he'd led the First Contact meetings with the Aldierrans. He'd been in charge of tricking them to end their war. He'd done the most research on the culture, which wasn't much but it was more than anyone else knew. Once they got settled in, the three of them would assemble individual teams as they spread out to supervise the world the best they could. Jae was the one who best knew right now what they should be doing.

Londo held his phone to his ear and waited for his adoptive father, Maximus, to pick up. "Hal, the sky's supposed to be green, we think," he said without preamble. "There are no birds in it. Rats enough in the street. Insects, but none of them pretty. Aldierran cockroaches, probably."

"Practically no women. I still haven't seen anyone laugh with joy," Jae told the phone from where he stood. "The kids I saw the other day ran in gangs."

Londo pointed. "Kids working," he said, though Jae couldn't see them. "Too young to be lugging around stuff like that." He winced, and the phone's camera caught it. "Fighting. Knives mostly."

"Well, stop it," his father told him.

"No, Hal," Jae said. "We do the big jobs. That will keep us busy enou–" His head jerked to the side, and he nodded to someone.

Londo turned. Admiral Bracken – no, not Admiral. Since the space navy had been so soundly trounced, he was now commanding the majority of planetary forces as "Field Marshal." He had emerged from the building, waving them in, three aides at his sides.

"Gotta go." Londo told Hal and clicked the phone off. The newcomers seemed awed to spot Lon and Jae. Well, good. That would help. Celebrity and respect usually resulted in cooperation.

If this meeting went the way Londo thought it would, things might need to get a bit… authoritarian around here. For a while at least. This kind of calamity couldn't be allowed, not when he was around.

Just as any Legion Team lieutenant would, Londo walked a pace behind and to the right of Jae as they entered the building.

Jae could tell that Londo was holding in his anger and frustration. Londo should let Jae do most of the talking here. Lon was the best at speeches, but Jae was a master of diplomacy, especially of the tricky kind.

The room they'd been led to was wide but low-ceilinged. No windows pierced the walls and lighting was, in Jae's opinion, surprisingly poor. Perhaps Aldierrans had better vision than he in dim lighting. A large picture of the Patriarch of Aldierra was the only touch of humanity on the walls. Other than that, they were lined with monitors that displayed troop positions, prison occupancy, weaponry distribution charts, and type too small and dark to make out from across the room.

The rectangular conference table was smaller than the one Jae had been at during his previous trip. Only ten men could fit around it. Others sat on chairs lining the walls or at monitor consoles. A few merely stood behind others in the role of aides. No chairs were set at the end of the table opposite the Patriarch, so that was where Jae and Londo stood.

No doubt that on top of everything else they needed to accomplish, Lon was redesigning the room in his head. Possibly the entire building. Probably the entire city. Lon was proud of his architecture and engineering licenses, but he also suffered from a slight case of claustrophobia, left from the long years he was kept imprisoned in a tiny room. He often daydreamed to offset the anxiety, but this place wouldn't help his mood. If irritated, Lon could be short with people.

A raised eyebrow in Lon's direction reminded his husband to pay attention.

Lon rubbed his new earring in consternation.

**Don't pick at it!** Jae commanded telepathically, and Londo stopped.

The marble-sized translator hovered next to him, pausing as it struggled with the new language. It delivered Jae's words to the group of uniformed men. The orange-skinned people came in all ages and shades of a skin hue that was brighter than Feithi or Terran norms. Their uniforms presented primarily in greens, with a few violet suits mixed in to signify allies. These were the high governors of the world, a stratocracy that had many factions violently working against it. Reds and blues, especially the blues, were enemies of the state.

Which didn't necessarily make them the bad guys.

Even so, everyone here deserved to breathe fresh air. Once again, Jae commanded the devas, or nature spirits, within the room to clear out the impurities, and he summoned more oxygen and nitrogen. He tweaked the room's decomposing organic compounds so they became inert, no longer contributing to the stale smell. No one else noticed but he saw they were all breathing better.

What he'd said hadn't sat well with the Patriarch, Lord Generalissimo Lupoff, a portly older man who turned a violent shade of rust when he was questioned by someone he considered an inferior. Which seemed to be everyone.

"We *are* working hard on this," Lupoff declared. His extra weight showed his status. Judging from the aides on the farthest sidelines, consumed calories equaled power. Lupoff also had six wives, another show of power on a world where women made up only one-fourth the population, as far as Jae had been able to discern.

"We have our forces spread all over the globe," Lupoff continued. "We are quelling the riots."

Jae didn't need to glance at Londo to feel him aiming an icy stare at the generalissimo to show how much he knew that was a lie.

"We're putting those who need it into mental facilities, as you suggested. Cleaning up our streets. Our roads have never been cleaner."

Jae scratched the back of his head. "It's not the streets we're particularly worried about, Excellency," he said. "It's *everything*. Together we made an agenda. What became of that?"

Lupoff huffed, "We have prioritized. It's a big world." He then proceeded to list in detail what his armies had done. He went through different territories. Continents. All of the actions either terrorized people in some fashion, imprisoned them, or… swept roads.

"Impressive enough," Jae lied. "You and your men have done this, but doesn't it seem… rather lacking in substance? In projects that will have a long-term effect?"

"We have only nine months before Doomsday!" one of the generals exclaimed.

They were calling it "Doomsday," as if inviting it to come. When Lina had channeled the planet to every Aldierran, every man here had had it imprinted upon his mind. Their world had spelled out what it was the humans were doing that was destroying her physically. She would not tolerate it anymore. If they didn't shape up with definitive plans and actions, she would destroy all her native humans in three seasons.

Then the Three Worlds of Aldierra, Sarastor and Earth, with Feith hovering in the background from whatever level of reality she and her population had evolved to, had Initiated Londo, Jae and Lina. They would oversee remaking these worlds into shining examples to the rest of the galaxy. They should help lift their populations to new levels of co-existence with their worlds and each other.

Jae nodded at the general. "Yes, only nine months until 'Deadline.' Not necessarily 'Doomsday,' so don't call it that, not even in your private thoughts. Words are powerful things. You also have twenty billion people to call upon. Twenty billion sets of ideas to work from. What are you doing to mine that?"

Lupoff nodded to Captain Liji, who stood from his favored position at the table. "We have impounded thousands from various professions. Ordered them to come up with plans. Our entire system awaits their input."

Lon wiped his hand down his mouth and looked at Jae. Jae tried to keep from showing his own impatience. After years of perfecting an impassive visage, it was difficult to accomplish this time.

This was not what they'd hoped would be done, not with a Deadline looming for the world. Time to switch to Plan B.

"So you're basically running in place while time ticks away," Jae decided to say. He tipped his head toward Lon, who nodded.

Londo gave it a moment and then stretched where he stood, commanding attention. This involved rolling his impressive shoulders and back, and flexing those arms that could stop starships in their tracks. His thighs expanded and contracted with the flux of pure power within.

Jae could almost hear sphincters clench around the room.

"Say," Londo ventured innocently. "What if we three Chosen of the Three Worlds helped investigate these ideas? Maybe coordinated in implementing the best of them as well?"

"You could concentrate on your usual duties," Jae told the group helpfully. "Give us the authority to act, to have others around the world act as well. Give us the power to help change your world for the better."

Lupoff chewed on that. "How much power?"

"We would clear everything through you first," Jae assured him even as his husband whispered, **Not likely,** in his mind.

"We wouldn't do a thing without your permission," Jae continued. "But perhaps three people can move more quickly than your armies."

Lupoff looked to Liji, then to the other high-ranking officials around the table. Then he eyed Jae and Londo, as well as peered around to see if a missing third person were there.

"This would include the Speaker?" he asked. "The woman?"

"It would. Aldierra will communicate with the Speaker, tell her what she needs, warn her if we're heading in the wrong direction. Your troops can't tap into those messages."

"A woman." Lupoff's mouth turned sour before his face relaxed in defeat. "What choice do we have?" His sharp eyes cut to his left, meeting the glance of another official. *Can we fight this?* he truly wanted to ask, but only Jae or Londo heard the unspoken words. The official shrugged, and Lupoff sighed.

Jae could feel Londo fiercely hiding a smile. **No bloodshed needed to get this deal. That's a relief,** Lon silently chortled as Lupoff granted his permission.

Jae ignored his husband. "Please make an official communication to that effect, Your Excellency. We can put out feelers today for what we think we'll be needing, you can keep gathering information and ideas, and in a week when this Mind Control Tour is over we'll be able to hit the ground running."

Londo and Lina walked through the hotel with their arms around each other as Lina finished the exciting tale of how she'd actually taught a hundred and forty students so far and had neither fainted nor thrown up. Well, past that first bathroom break when she'd done a quick upchuck before getting back to work. Efficient, that's what it had been, she thought proudly.

"Told you you could do it," Londo said. He disengaged long enough to pull out her chair at the bistro's table.

Lina regarded the unfamiliar action with puzzlement for a moment before sitting. Ah, etiquette based on gender. She'd get used to this as well, though she might have to set rules on some of the sillier bits. Lon had been her first boyfriend, the first person in years she'd been able to touch. She had so little experience in these things!

"You can do anything you set your mind to. A hundred and forty! Plus all the zombies."

He had such faith in her. If Lina hadn't already been so warm just by being near her new husband, she would have noticed the additional flush from gratification at his words.

They both looked up as Jae slid into the seat next to her at the table. He'd reported in for the two Legionnaires once they'd ported back from Aldierra. "Chim says that the first session was a resounding success." His smile beamed at her and he squeezed her hand between his, but didn't do anything more. They were in public. "Congratulations. I told you so."

Jae was so wonderful as well.

"Here you are." Er'k Gallad, the redheaded Legionnaire known as Sunstorm and the newest member of Jae's Alpha Team, reported from behind Jae's right shoulder. Two other Legionnaires accompanied him.

"Erik!" Lina exclaimed in delight. She could never get his name quite right, but he said he was okay with her garbled version. Thank goodness. "They've got you working too?"

He gave her a quick grin of hello before he passed Jae a notepadd. Jae checked it, then let Londo read the screen. Jae reported, "Food prep reports a go for the second session. Good thing, as the crowd seems to have eaten everything we brought in, enough for…"

"The zombies were hungry," Lina told them.

She felt like dissolving into pleased giggles. She wasn't even dreading the second workshop of the day. Miracle! With both husbands here she finally felt as if she could draw a deep breath, maybe even relax for lunch. Or was it dinner?

They were ignoring this world's diurnal cycles. The Tour would operate within its own time. They began right after breakfast, then when the first class of seven to eight hours was over, they went to lunch/dinner. Then another class, another meal, call it what you wished, and then everyone was scheduled for bed. Stimulants would be needed to stretch their days. Windowless rooms might also lessen the strain to the staff's brains. The hotels involved agreed to reset their interior lighting to reflect the Tour's schedule.

They all were determined to accomplish this.

After more congratulations and small talk, the Legionnaires left. Jae's face turned solemn. "Here's what we learned on Aldierra. The Council says they've been working hard on plans, but they're not ready to tell us what they are yet, not for a few more days."

"Not even a hint?" Lina asked around a mouthful of soggy bluish stuff. If you disregarded the texture, the taste wasn't that bad. Not particularly good either. "They only have nine months. Every day counts."

"We went to Plan B. Got permission to start doing what we want, without the military's approval," Lon told her before turning to Jae. "Let me talk personally with Bracken next time." That low tone of his held such promising menace. Londo didn't need to demonstrate his megaparastrength to strike fear into his enemies.

Bracken had been in charge of the invasion operation, the one weeks ago that had tricked the Mega-Legion into leaving Sarastor. The trick that had ended when the Legionnaire Aiko had been killed. It was agonizing for Lon to think of the woman who had loved him so dearly. How he wished he could have reciprocated to the same extent. He had tried. She had died in Londo's arms, professing her love for him. They'd given her the hero's funeral she deserved. "This is no time for them to be effing around, playing games. Twenty billion people. Bracken will help us. He knows he has a lot to make up for."

The men both focused on Lina as they felt her reaching for the consciousness that was the actual world of Aldierra.

**It is the humans' decision,** the planet told her. She let Jae and Londo hear the echo. **If they do not wish to act, then that shows a bad attitude. But consider: the general populace received the Ultimatum as well as the Council. If they see the Council not acting, maybe that will give them more impetus to act themselves. If they decide to. Do this Tour, Speaker, and help the children of our other sisters out there. We all approve of this. It will not take overlong to accomplish, and it will set many minds and hearts at ease.**

Londo put his elbows on the table, lay his chin on his clasped hands, and gazed into the distance. He looked at the both of them. "At least we know the Worlds are still in favor of us doing this Tour," he said. "So let's do it and get it over with and let the Council have these six days to institute whatever plan they come up with. Bracken's *kicking* cunning, but I think he's basically honest in this. At least he knows that the threat is real and that we're on his side. He'll tell us if they're trying to trick the planet."

Jae shrugged agreement. "It's too bad the Worlds didn't start us off earlier. The Tour's going to take up all Lina's schedule and then some for a few days. I think that by tonight we'll be pretty busy here as well."

"What's tonight?" Lina asked, looking back and forth at them.

Jae took a sip of her tea and considered it, then took a longer drink. "By tonight they'll" and he made a whirling gesture with his index finger to include worlds upon worlds Out There, "have figured out that, (A) you can do what you claim, (B) you're teaching a lot of important people who can get the word out, and (C) certain people are going to be out of business if they don't put *you* out of business."

"Don't worry about it," Londo said quickly as Lina went pale.

"We are the Legion," Jae said. He picked up a pile of baked vegetables from Londo's plate. His sfork tracked a wavy motion in the air as he made his point. "Every bit of our reputation is earned. The Legion's got security on the Tour and we've tied it in with the best security this planet's got to offer. No one's going to get through again. Eat." He held the sfork in front of Lina's face, and she hesitated, then opened her mouth for it.

"Watch it," Londo said softly, and the gentle smile on Jae's face slid away. They were in a public place, after all.

"Sorry," Jae muttered. "I haven't learned my role yet."

"No harm done," Lon told him and passed him a helping for himself.

"At least that had some texture to it," Lina said to relieve the tension. "It's much better than the mush I was eating. We're getting paid for doing this, right? There's some kind of fund people are paying into to attend? Should we even be charging for something like this?"

Without waiting for the answer Jae seemed ready to provide, she went on. "I suppose so. The Tour's going to give us money we can use on the Aldierran project." She heaved a sigh. "I'm a part of this. I should be keeping an eye on expenses too. Exactly how much money are you two putting into this? This is a really nice hotel. It must be costing a fortune."

"Don't worry about it," Lon assured her. "We'll fill you in when this is all over. I think Wiley has information on income from the Tour. Maybe Stoan or Andri. It should be a good amount. So many worlds are desperate for this."

"We're going to need a desperate amount of money for Aldierra," Jae muttered.

Lina asked, "How do interstellar payments work, anyway? Will AffSys money be recognized there? And vice versa?"

Until the attempted invasion, far-off Aldierra had been unknown to the Affiliated Systems. The two men made notes on their padds to find the answer to that question.

As they eased back to a less business level of talk, Lina began to worry about security. Just a few days ago Londo had placed her in Olympia's care while he went to fight that quick war. Now the legendary Earth hero was cocooned in a medical wing in Legion Headquarters on Sarastor, awaiting complete body reconstruction. The rogue Galactic Guardian, Paul Granger, had beaten her to a pulp using his Ruby and the power it funneled from the dark hole in the center of the galaxy. He'd raped her as well and had tried twice to rape Lina. He'd come so close.

She shivered as the cold terror of the moment roiled around her again. It seemed that the fist-sized Ruby secured next to her heart turned to ice as well.

"What is it?" Jae asked. He reached for her hand but stopped.

Instead Londo wrapped her hand in his. "Tell us about it, *chérie*. We'll go somewhere private. You still haven't told us all the—"

"No." Lina shook the panic away from herself and sat up straighter. "No, that's all right. The Legion will protect us, I'm sure. I'm just a little tired. I'll be needing a stim sometime during the next class, and I bet the others will too. One of those timed ones. Who can do that? There's a Legion doctor here, right? I can't remember if we've arranged that already." One would think the possibility of having another poison scare would keep her awake.

"You've got to talk it out sometime," Jae insisted.

"And this isn't a good time, is it? The next class starts in an hour. I need to meditate at least a few minutes before then. And I want to speak with the Tishana. I mean, I don't even know all their names yet. That's not good. One of them came up with a really good trick during the last class, too. Maybe if we work together, we can figure out a way to do this quicker, more efficiently."

"Don't worry about security, *chérie*. We've got it covered."

She tried to give Londo a trusting smile. "I know. Oh, Dinah!" she called as her friend passed their table. "Come sit with us for a minute."

The woman paused more than a second.

"They don't bite," Lina said.

"Unless invited." Jae grinned at Dinah and she eased onto a chair.

"Um. Valiant. Neutrino."

"This is Londo and Jae," Lina prompted. "My friend Dinah Stewart, one of volunteers to help me during the Tour."

Dinah looked cross-eyed at her. "Well, duh. We all met them last night, remember?"

"Right," Lina laughed. "But now he's Londo; he's Jae; got that?"

"Londo Starhart," Lon said.

Lina could practically see him chewing over his new last name. She knew this name would be unfamiliar to those billions who had known of him as Londo Rand for all these years, but people would just have to adjust.

"Starhart," Dinah said. A lighter-skinned woman, she had medium-length, curly brown hair and relied on more eyeliner and flashier clothing than normal in order to look exotic. It was part of her self-marketing as a professional psychic. "That's so cool, that you did it. And it's a cool name, I mean. And you–" she turned suddenly to Jae. "The Tishana say you're the Last Feithi and that means that you're practically a saint or something."

"I'd hardly call him a saint," Lon said.

"Or something," Dinah said in her defense.

"It just means that I'm the last of my kind," Jae said, and his eyes flicked for a moment to Lina. To Lina that simple glance carried a world of expectations for the future: a happy marriage with children. Jae scratched his chest. "Feith was a very advanced world."

"And you're the last one," Dinah said. "You can control matter or something."

Lina leaned forward. "So you've been talking with the Tishana? What are they like? Who should I start with if I want to get to know them?"

"Oh, them. They're all telepaths – 'teeps,' I mean, that's so cool – did you know that? There's a school there that actually teaches you how to become a teep. Mar-yo, he's the one with the purple eyes – not violet; bright purple! – he seems to be in charge, or maybe he's second in charge. Come to think of it, purple is the color for being in charge. I'll have to check his aura, see if it's purple too."

"Did you know the Tishana can *see* Sue's hoops of light?"

"No! Actually see them?"

"Yes. But they don't use any guides."

"Wh–? How can anyone worth their salt not use guides? And angels?"

"Different frequencies?"

Dinah made a rude noise. "Dumbasses, maybe. But Mar-yo's not a dumbass. He'll talk to you when the others won't."

"Mar-yo." Lina scanned the crowded tables.

"There." Dinah whispered in her ear as she pointed him out. "The cute one. Just look at him. Couldn't you just eat him up? I think he's single, but I don't know for sure." Mar-yo was slender, dark, and held a sour expression.

"Erik's here as part of Legion security," Lina said. "You remember him, don't you?"

"Erik?" Dinah was thoughtful for a moment and then her eyes brightened. "Oh, you mean tall, red-headed and hot? Oh wow, I guess he *would* be one of these, ah, Legionnaires, wouldn't he?"

"That's the one. He's so nice. He liked you."

"He did? He *is* a Legionnaire, though? Where's he now?"

"He just left. I think he's on duty. He might be in one of the classes because he's on Jae's team. That's a Legion Alpha Team." Lina regarded her husband with pride. Both of them led Alpha Teams.

But Londo was making yappy-motions with his hands, "talking" back and forth behind their backs, to Jae's amusement. Lina gave him a warning look before turning back.

"He's not a Team Leader, so he shouldn't be an attendee," Jae said to cover their inattention. "But since the war here we know he's a teep–"

"I think he should be called psi sensitive," Lina corrected. "He could develop into a telepath if he trained."

"Whatever. I think Stoan's slipping him into one of the sessions. As a guard, if nothing else."

"Oh good!" Dinah exclaimed. Her gaze moved from Jae to something behind Lina.

Lina didn't have to turn. She could feel the presence of the Dark Force, even if a soundtrack didn't come on the room's speakers with heavy breathing.

"Stoan," Jae said mildly.

The Legion commander moved around so Lina could see him. He was as amazingly tall as most people Out Here, with ultramarine skin that made him seem cold. His ultra-short hair was a dark, grayish blue, and his physique was chiseled, like his Sculptor hadn't lingered to soften many edges. "Psyche reported that this morning's workshop went well," he said.

"Psyche" was Chimrin, the ex-Commander.

As if he almost couldn't bring himself to say the words, he managed, "There were good results."

Did she really have to speak to him? Such a jerk. "Yes," Lina decided to say. "We got one hundred and forty 'good results.'"

His lips tightened. "We'll get another one hundred and forty in this next session?"

"Yes. We will."

Staredown.

"Lina's doing a great job," Jae put in, possibly with too much forced lightness. "After this is over, we should hold a party."

"Jae will personally act as bartender, won't you?" Londo asked.

"Absolutely."

Stoan looked from one Legionnaire to the other, especially at Londo's hard gaze on him, warning him off. The commander let out something between a grunt and a puff of air and moved along.

"Gotta fix that," Jae mumbled.

It was a definite grunt that signaled Londo's agreement. "Down, girl," he told Lina.

"Well," Lina said as her muscles relaxed again. Dinah was looking confused at the confrontation. "Well. Dinah, could you introduce me to Mar-yo?"

"Sure, Lie. But you have to let me hang around Erik during his session. Come with me."

# 4

The day before, Dinah and the rest had gathered in Sue Taylor's basement at Lina's call. They all still lived in the general Durham area where they'd taken Sue's wide-ranging psychic lessons every Thursday night for three years. Originally those classes had been jammed shoulder-to-shoulder with students – then-touch-phobic Lina almost succumbed to panic in more than a few classes – but by the time they finished, there were just the seven of them, with three being natural telepaths of varying strength.

They'd been taught the history of psi work, as well as numerous specialized techniques from pendulums to the healing methods of Ko-Laimni and Reiki, to introductory massage, homeopathy, past life regressions, and more. Sue's then-boyfriend, David Autry, had introduced them to the tarot and astrology. Sue was delighted that Lina could teach them all clairvoyance, since she'd arrived as a self-trained expert. As time passed, Sue asked Lina to instruct a few independent psychic classes that she'd scheduled but couldn't attend for one reason or another.

They'd graduated and set off to begin their own careers as part-time psychics. But they retained their connections, encouraging each other when necessary, and sharing hints as to how to run a profitable business.

"Look at you!" Sue shrieked when she hugged Lina and Lina didn't pull away. "Dinah said you'd gotten over that touch phobia. I didn't believe it."

Sue's basement was as familiar as home. Throw rugs tried to cover up the cement floor, but there was no hiding the furnace and water purification system in the back corner. Sofas and side tables that had been collected off street curbs made for a comfortable atmosphere. The group carefully rearranged crystals and candles on tabletops to make room for paper plates of store-bought cookies, finger snacks, and paper cups of iced tea that Lina had brought with her.

Lina laughed. "Londo did it. We're not quite sure how, but we were sharing minds and he did… well, something. It involved past lives. And more. And him. His heart, I mean. He's a really caring man. He worked hard on me getting to…"

"Oh yeah, hard," Yej Ham crowed. The others chuckled, except for Elena, who hid her smile behand her hand.

"No! Sheesh," Lina muttered. "He was trying to get me to the point where I'd accept his proposal, and–"

"Wait, you turned him down?" David asked, his eyes wide. David took pains to look like The Authority In All Things, but this news was beyond his efforts.

"At first. Maybe a few times. But somewhere in there he got my phobia to go away by accident. Ninety-five percent of it, anyway. I think it'll disappear completely in time."

"Whoa." Dinah crunched noisily on some nachos.

"But that's not why we're here," Lina insisted. She explained the dangers of galactic Mind Control to the group.

"Hooks?" Cartrell Page asked. Lina had been pleasantly surprised she'd been able to lure him away from a gaming tournament. He was a national champion at, oh, some game she wasn't familiar with. It was violent; she knew that much. "I've worked with a few. Are you talking about the same thing I'm thinking of?"

"Big hooks," Lina said. "Lots of big, crafty hooks. With some sinister thin ones worked in that are the hardest of all to extract. They're wielded by bad people who know exactly what they're doing. They've added technology to the mix."

"Hooks that cause trouble," Sue mused. "I usually do what I can and have the person come back a few times to see if multiple sessions will work better. Sometimes I smudge them."

"I light lots of candles and we pray," Depika suggested. She could be intense in her concentration, but her motives were always pure.

"Does it work?"

The group muttered, some shrugging. The consensus was that their techniques helped a little. Hooks weren't usually that bad, as people on Earth weren't specifically trained and modified to be Mind Controllers. Then again, controlled people didn't usually seek remedy.

"Well, I came up with a way to do it," Lina told them. "About a year or so ago, I got this one woman in who was just covered with thick hooks. Her husband was a crazy bastard. He controlled everything in her life. Her daughter was the one who almost forcibly brought her to me. She could barely think for herself. I had to figure out something right then and there, before her husband came back from a business trip. It worked very well on her, and ever since then it seems that I get a badly hooked person every other week. I don't know where they came from. I tried some more tricks, found out what works and what doesn't."

Lina gave them a ten-minute synopsis of what she was doing before she asked, "How would you all like to go Out There for six days and help me teach? I'm not sure how much we could pay, but we'd make it worth your while. We leave tonight. They're really hurting."

"Out… There?"

"You mean, space?"

"The final frontier," Lina said. "We'll furnish translators. Rooms and meals. I'm not sure how much sightseeing you'll be able to do, but if you can't do it during the Tour, Lon and Jae say they can arrange for you to visit some of the worlds afterward, if you want."

"Jae? Who's—"

"Oh yeah, Jae." Lina thought for a moment before saying, "When you first see him, don't stare. Everyone stares."

"Is he… deformed?"

"Big nose? Three eyes?"

Lina reached for the padd in her pocket and brought up a holo picture of Jae on it.

The women in the group, even Yej, exclaimed in wonder and profanity. The men, both straight, were silent but awed.

"Is he—"

"No, Dinah, he's taken. Unavailable. However, there will be lots of hunky Legionnaires around. Male and female. All the Alpha and Beta Team Leaders are required to take the class so they can teach it to their teams. Lon and Jae are Alpha Team Leaders. I'm not sure how many of the Gamma Team Leaders will be there.

"Six days. We can cover your rent and utilities and pet sitting… and childcare, Elena, in addition to a salary. You'll have to sign some kind of paperwork, I'm not sure, but the doctors Out There are great. They can handle almost anything. More than likely we'll be needing stimulants for the long hours to handle everyone. Stims are great; no side effects unless you practically overdose on them. We'll have a doctor with us. Lon says he's got a lawyer if you want one to look over things. Who's game? I need all the help I can get."

The tight-faced Tishana who had shown up to help were frigidly polite as they waited for the next class to begin. Lina made some small jokes and laughed at them herself since they didn't. Dinah added a few encouraging chuckles of her own at what might have been punchlines, and two of the Tishana managed to loosen the sides of their mouths into some semblance of smiles.

Lina asked Mar-yo about the Tishan way to deal with the Mind Controlled, which seemed to be to lock zombies into hyperspace chambers and leave them. This shut off telepathic contact with a Controller until such time that the Controller lost interest in the Controlled and cut their ties. Sometimes hyperspace imprisonment lasted a lifetime.

Here on Deseed there were thousands of zombies in quarantine camps that were now blanketed with the broadcasts of psychic suppressor globes that Wiley had invented for the occasion. Emperor Yanist-Glory had tried to take over this world, but the Affiliated Systems Megaforce Legion and Earth's ParaNet had waged a days-long war last week that had successfully countered it. Now there were all those zombies to de-zombify, plus a few more yet to be caught. The hope was that students from this class would teach others on Deseed, who'd teach others. Eventually everyone could be returned to normal. Other students would fan out across the galactic sector to make sure the threat of Mind Control could never be used again.

Lina listened closely and asked questions whenever any of the Tishana paused, and then would ask a more personal question, mainly about something they wore, admiring it for whatever reason. Sometimes it was tough making new friends, especially when they didn't want to be. She didn't have Dinah's knack of flirting her way through a conversation.

A gong sounded as warning that the second class of the day was about to begin. Lina grabbed a jug of water that had a Legion seal on it and took off to meditate for a few minutes to bring her mind back to clarity and calm. With that done, she began teaching again.


By the middle of Day Two the Tour had gone from being vaguely frightening for Lina to being a kind of rush, a thrill as people pointed at her and deferred to her and she heard her name on everyone's lips. After that it devolved into damned hard work.

But it had been the very first class that second day that brought trouble. The Tishana had gathered around Lina before the session when she was trying to meditate, to offer suggestions about improvements. Lina's Terran friends had their own ideas. She set up a plan to test the two theories: one in the morning session, the other in the afternoon, side by side with her normal way so the group could see which worked best.

Satisfied, the assistants patiently supervised as the new students went through the routines again. By now they all thought they had Lina's spiel down by heart, but then they noticed that something was different.

In one of the smaller practice groups Lina had spoken with one of the Legionnaires she knew, Brügz Sikrichat, aka Ion Emperor. A few minutes later some of the auditorium's more sensitive participants murmured. One threw up, but each seat had come equipped with a barf bag for just such events. Brügz had turned on a telepathic damper whose field enveloped the auditorium. Until this session use of the damper had been saved for the second half of the lengthy class with its zombies.

Luckily, Lina had given her assistants a quick warning so they could steel themselves. Even so, two of the Tishana also had to vomit into their bags.

"This is to focus anyone who might want to cheat or take a shortcut," she told the class. They had just finished feeling each other's auras in preparation for a chakra balance. "Now we can concentrate more easily on some fine details. I think I need someone to show one little peculiarity of this balance. Could I get a volunteer? Or are you all too shy? Let me pick someone, someone... How about you?" She smiled at a woman standing in the front row, ignoring two hands that went up elsewhere. "This is a little trick that we all need to be aware of. Do you mind?" She held out her hand in encouragement, and the woman stepped uncertainly onto the stage.

"This is just like back home, when we watch magicians – and I mean entertainment illusionists, not the real thing – work. They always ask for an unsuspecting audience member, and the volunteer gets a nice round of applause after it's all over."

Lina turned to the audience. "I'd like you to consider our volunteer here. If you'll all center yourselves, use your natural psychic abilities to imagine my aura, imagine her aura..."

The woman let out a low growl, and Lina gritted her teeth in concentration as she pattern-tapped her right earring. "See? She's attempting to hook me. Wiley? Can you hear me? Can you put this up on the room screen so everyone can see?"

From wherever Dr. Mem-Bazer was outside the arena, the lecture viewscreen lit up with enhanced visuals of what was taking place on stage. A woman who Lina thought was a Legionnaire started to come up, but Lina waved her off.

"Look at the technique involved. So even if you have a telepathic damper covering an area like this room, someone can still try to place hooks in you by using psychic techniques. They can't focus it into Mind Control until after they're out of damper range, but the hooks can be implanted. If I concentrate on strengthening my throat chakra and solar plexus chakra... Oh, look, she's trying for the third eye chakra. You're so not getting in there."

The woman stood clenching her fists, concentrating fiercely as Brügz re-entered the back of the auditorium. He carried one of Wiley's telepathic inhibitor shackles.

The intensity of the hatred behind the woman's eyes made Lina pause. She flashed back to that ghastly night. A month ago, Lon's enemy, Terry Rhodes, had

stared at her in precisely that way as lasers had drilled into Lina's arm. The agony…
the sheer terror… Lon had been so near death and she'd been helpless…

No. That was then. This was now. Now. She had a job to do.

Lina blew the fear away with a determined breath.

She hoped no one had spotted her moment of inaction. "You can deflect the hook
as it's coming toward you," Lina instructed as the people in the audience stood with
their mouths open. Someone was actually trying to take over Lina Starhart!

"You catch them. You might imagine yourself catching a javelin or spear, or just
deflecting them with your hands." She illustrated with the hooks the woman tried on
her. The memory of Terry Rhodes' cruelty faded. Slightly. "Watch where you deflect them to, though. You don't want them landing on anyone by accident. Work
with intention. Make it deflect so that it disintegrates. You have no power here, not
over me, not over anyone else."

Brügz flew to the stage and clamped the long shackle on the woman's arm as her
attention was riveted on Lina. It clicked shut. The woman crumpled to the floor.

Lina did a final banishing gesture. "Thank you, Ion Emperor. Now, if everyone
will look at this woman's aura, note the difference between now and as she was. See
how the inhibitor practically shuts down the third eye, how the flow down from the
crown chakra is greatly depleted. That's what causes her to faint. Let me warn you
that she'll likely vomit – enthusiastically – once the inhibitor is taken off. As many
of you have noticed, this is an unfortunate side-effect for many of those innocents
who have to wear inhibitors to stop someone from Controlling them.

"But look at her and see this geometric pattern of puddles of black in her aura…"
Lina pointed them out on the screen as well as around her to her audience, explaining
what those meant and what to look for in others.

She'd never seen such before, but she could guess the relationship to what Wiley
and Chim had told her about the way unscrupulous people fiddled with people's
minds and brains Out Here. The woman was an artificial telepath. The machinery in
her brain left telltale signs. Lina reminded the audience that only artificial telepaths
and psychics who had had their empathy centers burned away were threats.

"We can surgically remove the implants now that she's wearing the inhibitor,"
Brügz explained. He signaled to the woman Legionnaire to come up and help him
carry her out of the room.

"That's what we're up against," Lina told her students. "As a good friend of mine
told me a few days ago, always check out a room that you're entering if you aren't
absolutely sure what you're getting into. Those of you who can see auras could tell,
once you knew what to look for, that she really stood out like a beacon in here. Me,

I usually don't see auras, but I've been immersed in giving this class for over a day now, so I'm more sensitive than normal."

"Then why didn't you get rid of her sooner?" a man in the audience asked.

"What, and lose a valuable learning experience?" Lina asked. "I think we'll have to make sure one of those comes to every class from now on. Just to keep us on our toes."

# 5

Reassured that such threats could be handled, Lina and her assistants breathed easier and could focus on their technique. One of the Tishana, Sweeney, tweaked hers, and Lina could see the improvement though she and the others weren't sure quite why it accomplished what it did.

"I just got a sudden inspiration," Sweeney said.

Good enough. It encouraged all to break out of their comfort zones. This was how new frontiers were discovered, Lina told herself as she tried to be more experimental too. When would be another time they'd have so many subjects to work on? As long as no one got hurt, and no one remained a zombie…

Jae attended the "afternoon" class as a Legion Alpha Team Leader. Lina made sure someone else handled the small practicing group he was put in. Working that closely with him in public, she'd surely give the game away.

Londo wanted their Triune kept secret until he could work up the nerve to publicly announce he was bisexual and in a marriage that most people would consider wildly abnormal. Lon had issues about friendships. He'd lost too many friends over the years due to dangerous situations. Now he didn't want to lose them because they disapproved of him.

Londo had been kidnapped by agents of the Empire when he'd been about three years old and kept among aliens who had experimented upon him. His only friend had been Ours the teddy bear, who eventually had been taken away. These days Londo treasured those who loved him.

Lina could understand that. Through the years she'd had friends, but Lon had been the first person who'd truly loved her. Then had come Jae, Lon's more-than-best friend. She wasn't going to give them up for anything.

The Tour attendees who were grouped with Jae tended to ease away from him with occasional low, awed bows in his direction. He was the Last Feithi after all, the sole survivor of a population that was held in reverence high above that of other humanity. They all had wielded awesome powers and displayed great elevation of spirit.

People respectfully bowed their heads to the various Legionnaires, Lina had seen, but for Jae they went practically into prostration. She saw him try to wave away the salutations, but some persisted as if unconsciously sensing the power of his personal aura.

Yet even the Last Feithi seemed puzzled and then surprised when, after the zombies had been de-zombified, the Terran delegation tried a new trick. The idea had come from both Elena, a devout Catholic, and Yej, a devout Pagan, who pooled their love of archangels into an idea.

Archangels were supremely powerful spiritual beings. Through the years Lina had worked with them, but she was still confused about where they were slotted into the Grand Scheme of Things. Some people thought they were vastly more important than mere humans and almost as powerful as Source, or God, while others thought that someday childlike humanity would rise to their levels. Others considered current humanity every bit equal to those of the angelic realm, only placed in a physical sphere in which almost all didn't recall their true being.

Someday Lina vowed to take much time to consider Source and Spirit. For the nonce she used the concepts in a utilitarian way.

She signaled the auditorium systems to wash the area in sapphire blue light. Then she called on the archangel Michael to wield his mighty sword to sever any connections these people might have in both present and past lives to people or ideas that did not serve them well. She asked Michael to watch over them as they returned to their lives, and to continue to protect them from those who might harbor ill will to them.

As the meditation ended, audible sighs came from across the chamber. Lina could feel a weight lift from the place. Even the Ruby on her chest seemed calmer than usual. She checked her assistants. Elena and Yej both had "told you so" expressions on their faces. The Tishana looked a bit blank, still absorbing it all. A couple moved to confer with each other.

She glanced to Jae, who raised his left eyebrow at her and nodded approvingly. She wrinkled her nose at him to get a quick grin in return. They would certainly keep that part of the process!

The seven-hour session had contained a few long snack breaks, but now that it ended the staff enthusiastically headed off for what they were calling "dinner." Jae and Lina joined Londo in the private, plush bistro reserved for the staffers. It was so lovely to be able to sit with her new husbands, even if the food wasn't much to talk about. Admittedly she spent the first few minutes admiring them and the rush of excitement within her they inspired, instead of listening. Jae had to repeat himself to her.

"You aren't looking into their faces," he told her.

Oh. He meant with the teaching.

"With everyone." He used an index and middle finger to point to her eyes and then to his. "Establish the connection."

"I've told her this before," Lon said as he watched the two.

"Yes, yes, look in their faces," Jae said. "But Lina, I want you to look into their eyes. See their souls. Make the connection to yours."

Whoa. When he did it… it was like intense magnetism, as if they were physically pulled together. And all around that… the sense of him. And her. Connecting in a quite un-spiritual way.

"Maybe not that much," Jae admitted, and he cut down his "volume." "But you get the gist."

Lina took a cleansing breath to ease back from his presence. "Namaste," she said.

She placed her palms together at heart level and bowed to him. "It means, 'I bow to you' and the meaning behind that is because I recognize the soul, the Source-energy in you that is shared within me."

Jae nodded. "'We are one.'" Then he made the gesture and bowed. "Namaste. We will begin to use it as a greeting. You too, Lon. But Lina, learn to look into people's eyes."

She heaved a sigh. "So much to learn. I'll try."

"Do or do not; there is no 'try,'" Lon replied automatically as he rehearsed the hand position and bow. *Star Wars* to him was what *Star Trek* was to Lina. But Lon had arrived at dinner with news of Aldierra. Even with a doomsday looming for the entire world, its military government was still dragging its feet.

"We'll definitely have to do more than lend a hand here and there," Londo growled. "This may turn out to be work. Hard work."

He and Jae grimaced at each other.

Lina couldn't imagine why the population, with whom she had personally spoken (or allowed the spirit of their world to speak with), wouldn't jump at anything they could do to help their situation. Aldierra had been chillingly specific in her threat. Poor, misused Aldierra.

Then again, the overall impression she'd received had been of a world at war with itself in far too many ways. Violence and fear pervaded its energy. Civil wars raged in every territory. The environment was in tatters. When Jae had sent video of Aldierra two weeks ago, he'd noted a total of eight women among the people he'd observed. He'd been mostly touring governmental locations, but still. Eight.

Small wars punctuated the society, growing to frightening levels and then petering out when another war broke out over there, and over there, and then over there. The world grieved the beautiful flora and fauna that had been extinguished by her humans. They left only piles of refuse and death to mark their path through history.

Yesterday Jae had spoken to some of their contacts there to send out more feelers to see who on Aldierra already had solid ideas about how to improve the place.

"There's no need to reinvent the wheel," Londo reminded them. "Somewhere, people have been working on the planet's problems, likely for centuries. We'll also need data on things like animal migration, ancient crops, weather patterns, how things were on the world before all this crap took hold." He rubbed his nose before attending again to his food. "Although you'd think the Council would have investigated these kinds of data by now.

"Don't forget the AffSys," Lina said. "There's got to be mounds of research as to what works to make healthy ecosystems. What about–"

They both turned to Jae, who was expecting the question. "I already have people looking into that. I've opened up the whole of Feithi information vaults to two dozen organizations, with instructions on them giving us reports on how the people of Feith cared for themselves and their environment."

"Wow," Lon said reverently. "I want to see that as well. Imagine!" He nodded as he smiled at Jae. "Glad to hear it." Until this, Jae had kept all Feithi records locked to outsiders. Not to them, of course, not since the morning they'd proposed marriage to Jae.

Lina looked down at her feet. "Hey, Deseed," she called to the planet. "Tell your sisters they really should have started this project about a generation or two ago. But we'll do our best," she quickly added.

Lon said he'd check with the Aldierrans about how the hiring for special global communications was going, as well as the construction of several satellites for the same. He raised an eyebrow at her expression. "*Quoi?*"

She blew a breath out through her nose. "It's just that… Well, I feel left out. I'm just itching to begin on Aldierra, to see what the heck things are like. I don't remember much from the Ultimatum except the Ultimatum itself.

"I remember that the people were, for the most part, just ordinary people trying to live and survive their lives, a general impression, but I don't know about specifics. Where are they keeping all the women? Have they told you that yet? I remember feminine energy, so there's got to be more than a handful there. How do people live?

What's their culture? Or cultures, since we're talking an entire world? Or their history? How the heck did they get this way? What kind of animals do they have? Or plants? What state are their oceans in? I want to know everything.

"You two…" She leaned back in her chair, pouting, "You get to do something. It's not fair."

Jae laughed while Londo leveled an index finger at her. "You are heading this Tour, *ma chérie*. That's more than enough. You'll get to Aldierra after this important work is finished. Keep your mind on that. Four more days, plus recovery time."

Jae nodded and then cocked his head at her. "You already know it's a dangerous place. 'Doom and gloom' is a good description of what I've seen. In two weeks, we'll probably be begging to get away from Aldierra," he predicted.

"No."

He shrugged. "It's going to be tougher than we dreamed."

He should know, after his days with that world's people and his limited survey of the environment.

"So I should enjoy these classes while they last." Lina heaved a theatrical sigh. "At least I know what I'm doing with them. Pretty much."

"No one likes operating in the dark, kitten," Londo said. "We'll do as much preliminary work as we can around our Legion duties here."

"We might have a way to bring you in. Maybe a worldwide broadcast? From us, not the Council?"

Londo considered Jae's idea as he rubbed his nose. "That makes a lot of sense. The sooner the better. Tomorrow."

"Even without specifics, you've already talked with them all," Jae reminded Lina. "That's a few billion more than we've met."

They had a point. "Nine months," Lina reminded them.

"Nine months," they both replied grimly.


For Lina Day Three began with an empty bed but a messaged request to port Jae to Aldierra for a meeting after she was up and about. She wondered how her dear pack of cats were doing and spared each of them a lingering thought and dose of loving energy. After that Lon needed a lift to some AffSys world she'd never heard of. He'd ordered extra-massive, uber-tech machinery for Aldierra.

"I have a feeling I'm going to be tearing down a lot," he told her as he ducked into their bathroom after his early shift. His uniform was filthy from his Legion duties, so he changed to a new one, talking to her with the door open. "I want to be able to build as well. I need something super-adaptable. We don't know what we're going to run into."

"Hammers and nails?" Lina asked, knowing that it wouldn't be anything like that.

He laughed as he emerged, combing his now-wet hair. Woof. "Three-D printers, I guess you'd call them. Equipment that can build an entire city block in a few hours, given that it's fed the right materials. Ah *oui*," he muttered, and made some notes on his padd. "Materials. We'll have to have something that can convert everything I destroy into raw materials. Maybe we won't have any waste. Huh. That would be good." He muttered to himself as he wrote.

"Just how much are you planning to build?"

"As much as we need." He only touched the tip of his nose as he considered, not the full-out, mashing rub that signaled that he was bothered by something, so it must not have been much of a problem. For Valiant. "A few neighborhoods here and there, most likely. *Euh,* maybe a town or two. As far as we can tell, Aldierra is pretty much covered with buildings. We'll need to clear spaces so nature can fill it in. Though I don't think it's as bad as Sarastor, which has no excuse. They only have three billion people. Well, natives. Most of Sarastor is abandoned, due to tech not requiring so much space for information systems, security, weaponry… You know how it is."

Lina did not, but she would learn.

"Some Aldierrans will have to leave their homes and businesses. We need to provide them a place to live." He smiled at the thought. "Someplace nice."

"Ah, your architecture degree comes into use."

"*Saadlair 'assah.* This might turn out to be a fun mission, this Doomsday/Deadline."

That brought a snort from Lina, but she ported him to his destination anyway.

The machinery was bought using Lon's and Jae's enormous bank accounts. As famous Legionnaires, their pockets were deep. Lina didn't know how deep. They'd have to have a money talk soon. She just hoped those accounts could stretch to handle whatever they'd need.

This was an entire world they were helping. After the Ultimatum's deadline had run out they'd have two more worlds to care for. How would they ever get it done, no matter how much money her husbands made?

It didn't take long for Lon to grab his purchases, which were kept in orbits for shipping, and boost them into hyperspace using just his mighty Valiant shoulders and flying ability. A critical nav app perfected his aim. The journey to Aldierra was parsecs long and would take days. At that time Lon's app would give him the exact coordinates from which to retrieve the equipment and tow it into normal space, then down to Aldierra.

Elsewhere, Jae proved himself the master of conference calls. On Aldierra he saw to gathering experts in ecosystems, water systems, weather control, and more aspects of that world whose functions had fallen apart. Both he and Lon coordinated with the Great Council… and spoke with Field Marshal Bracken separately. By the time Jae was ready to port back by "lunch," the military had major divisions now truly focused on infrastructure and staffing for the network the Three Worlds needed to coordinate efforts. There were also scores of civilian groups working on the Three Worlds' agenda.

"How are we paying for the civilians?" Lina asked her husbands.

It was Lon who replied. "Bracken assured us that money is a mere concept."

"Surprisingly existential of him," Jae said.

"And also that Aldierra's military stretches far and has many lax points in its structure. Any real money these groups need is going to be finagled through them."

"Although since money is a mere concept, there won't be any losses for anyone to complain about. This will work… for now."

"Later though…" Londo mused.

"We'll need money."

"Any archangels in charge of financial concepts?" Jae asked Lina.

She thought. "I rarely work with the angels except for standard Michael protections when I do card readings. It's been a long time since I took that course on archangels. I should review it. It was really good. I have it in my Dropbox if you guys want to use it.

"Let's see… Ariel loves to hand out prosperity. And, and… Does Uriel? I should know that; I'm ordained in his order. Hey, you two are as well."

Jae's forehead furrowed. "It was always just the Order of Uriel. I knew he was some kind of good energy, but suppose I was too young to be told more. He's always been just a name attached to a vow of aiding others."

Londo merely shrugged. "I got ordained so I could perform our marriage. And do that other required stuff, helping people. Which I already was. So Uriel's an archangel?" He peered over Jae's shoulder as Jae searched his padd for information.

She frowned at them. This was important stuff they all should know. Uriel… Uriel… "He's the guy, all in gold, who can shower people with… Epiphanies."

"Not money then."

"All that gold confused me. No, Ariel's the one for that. Uriel helps us achieve our goals. We have a fairly large one ahead of us. He deals with transformations of all kinds."

"Here we go," Jae mused as he read Lina's notes. "Uriel. Claircognizance, helping achieve goals, practical solutions, renews faith, inner peace. Weather. Turns disappointments into victories. All excellent things, but no money here." He wrinkled his nose. "Feith wasn't into money. Our end goal is to transform Aldierra victoriously," he said solemnly. "Please invoke him as well as Michael."

"You can too," she replied. "Archangels are accessible to everyone. Guardian angels also, who are every bit as powerful as archangels." At Lon's questioning look, she added, "They're used mostly in children's stories so they've been fluffified and diminished. They aren't."

"Here's Ariel," Jae announced as he got to that section. "She carries around bags of coins and hands them out. Abundance, prosperity, courage. Ah, we'll be calling on her a lot to help with the flora and fauna of the world, which she also commands, so maybe we shouldn't stretch our luck by asking for money?"

"We can always ask. 'Thoughts become things,' as the saying goes."

"What saying is that? I've never heard it," Lon said.

"You don't run around in the proper New Age circles," Lina chided. "All humans have the power to manifest. We should start visualizing success. Just the end product, not the how it'll be accomplished. Mustn't limit what the Universe will do."

"But what if we're the 'how' in how it will be accomplished?" Jae asked as he returned his padd to his pocket.

"Do not try to confuse me," Lina replied loftily. "We should certainly ask the angels for help, ask them to enlist other angels as well." She glanced to the heavens and looked all around, beyond just Londo and Jae sitting there. "Please help us and our cause. Thank you." She closed her eyes with an inward smile. "I visualize success, a world reborn. So much good energy being put to use. People so happy. Aldierra celebrating and blooming with joy. Thank you, angels. Thank you for lending your power to this project. Thank you, Universe."

Lon cocked his head at her contented sigh. His gaze went to Jae, who held a thoughtful expression before he realized Lon's scrutiny. He nodded at his husband.

"We all need our own transformations," he said. "Any help is welcome."

So Londo silently asked any and all angels, including this Uriel fellow and Ariel whatever, to help them. It couldn't hurt.

"This or even better. Thank them as if it were accomplished," Lina told them.

"Time is unreal," Jae added. "The future is now. On a level we cannot see, the Deadline has arrived and passed."

Lon withheld his mutter about what he thought about *that* and did as told.


Stoan's arms remained crossed as he and fellow Legionnaires watched the crowd emerge from the session.

"I don't care," he declared. "I don't trust this. It's too easy."

"It's remarkably easy," Chimrin replied from his side. She'd been Legion Commander when Stoan had still been a new Alpha Team Leader. "And yet complicated. It requires a… distinctly unusual way of looking at human energies."

"But it does work? Completely?" Brügz Sikrichat, Chimrin's ex-husband and the commander just before Stoan, asked. "We sure could have used this during the Dubblest crisis."

"It does," his ex replied. "I've monitored them. The entire Tishana delegation has performed deep scans on them all. We concur."

The cured zombies were hugging each other, shouting their joy at permanent freedom, dancing in delight. The personnel assigned to checking their names off lists were having difficulty getting them to calm enough to give them further information.

By now there were banks of communications equipment placed for the ex-zombies' use. Call after call went out. To homes, to family, to loved ones.

After that the transportation managers stepped in to send these people to the ones who'd been waiting for them for so very long. Even now, on the third day of the Tour, the entire staff was exultantly surprised by the results that emerged from the auditorium.

"We should be just as happy," Subcommander Nurunori, aka Andri, told her commanding officer. "I think you should be smiling. Maybe take a moment to relax?"

"I don't trust it, not any of it."

Andri and the others exchanged glances around him. The right half of Chimrin's mouth turned up. "You will. Stubborn *beggle.* You're still stuck on your own history with Mind Control. It's over. Now it seems, it's *all* over, or it soon will be."

Brügz let out a snort. "People will find some other way to enslave. They always do."

Everyone sighed in agreement.

"But for today," Stoan said hesitantly, "maybe we can take a breath. Just today."

Chimrin nudged him with her elbow. "There may be hope for you yet."

They might have chuckled, but Alpha Team member Mimik was approaching. It was always difficult to tell her expression since she was a humanoid insect. Her tall lankiness invoked a Terran praying mantis, but her body possessed more heft and she held herself proudly. Her skin was beautifully mottled with spring greens, subdued emerald and olive, with a surprising splash of salmon here and there that Stoan believed was cosmetic. She had four arms but only three fingers and a thumb on each hand, which still resulted in more digits than most humans possessed. She came from four sectors over, far from the shared evolutionary wave of Sarastor's and its neighbors' sectors. Her movements now were sharp, which meant she was worried, and she glanced behind herself with her large pearlescent eyes as she came near.

"If I could have a private word, Commander?" She nodded respectfully at the others, and they stepped away.

"What's up?" Stoan asked her when they had a fair-sized empty space around themselves. He signaled his Legion Array to encase them in a no-communications zone. The world around them shifted into a blur.

Even so, Mimik seemed nervous. "I didn't want to say anything before. Even now I'm not sure."

Stoan made an encouraging noise.

"You know I have to be expert in human expressions. To be able to disguise myself as human."

"You're the best, Mimik. We know that."

"I've been seeing. I hate to do this. He's so respected. He's a symbol. A legend."

"Go on." It was unlike Mimik to be so reticent. She was Alpha Team.

"It's Neutrino."

Stoan came to instant attention. "What about him? Do you think he's Controlled?"

"He's… He's looking at Mrs. Valiant in odd ways. Ways I usually assign among humans to romantic feelings. As opposed to lustful ones, though now and then… Let's just classify them for now as romantic. It's odd."

Not if it was what Stoan was thinking. "Why?"

Mimik settled her shoulders to another angle, as if doing so helped her to put her words together. "Neutrino has expressions."

Stoan managed a chuckle. "Yes. He likes to pull his two expressions. I think he thinks they make him look mysterious. Maybe inscrutable."

"I've counted six expressions in his formal repertoire, with a possibility of two more." Mimik bowed her head slightly to Stoan. "But that's likely because I'm very good at what I do."

"Ah, there's that Alpha Team confidence," Stoan said with a quick grin. "Six, you say?"

"I believe he uses them when he needs to mask what he's truly feeling. I find he's been using them a lot lately, and in settings one wouldn't expect them. Settings where Valiant or. Perhaps I should say 'and/or.' Valiant and/or Mrs. Valiant are nearby."

"But when he's not using his expression repertoire…" Stoan prompted. When Jae wasn't controlling himself…

"He gives her looks. He makes significant looks in her direction, even when she is not looking back."

"Looks."

She added, "And Mrs. Valiant returns the same expressions, with or without him seeing her."

Stoan rocked on his heels and pursed his lips. "Ah," he managed to say.

"This doesn't come as a surprise to you?" Mimik's head tipped to her left as she gave him one of those scouring examinations she was known for.

"Let's just say…" Stoan chose his words carefully. "I'd like you to keep an eye on this. On both of them."

"I will not have Londo hurt," Mimik declared. "He's not only my Team Leader but my friend."

"Understood." Stoan shifted. "Tell me, how does Mrs. Valiant look at her new husband?"

Mimik shook her head. "This is what baffles me. She clearly adores him. I don't see any artifice in it." The whistling sound she emitted could have been a frustrated chuckle or a huff. "And he's smitten with her. It's obvious, even to you, I'd think. Not at all like it was between him and… and Aiko."

Just three weeks ago Stoan had had to pry Aiko's body out of Lon's arms. Lon had not wanted to let the impaled heroine go, to admit she was dead.

"Yes."

"She was completely taken with him but didn't get an equal amount of affection from him in return. I believe he tried to love her. He did, but not…"

"You got all of this from his body language?"

Mimik gave an exaggerated tip of her head to Stoan that even a human could understand, accented with the tiniest of eye rolls. "We are good friends. Friends talk, especially when duty carries long hours and the subject of such talk is far away."

"I see." Stoan stood for a few moments more and Mimik waited. "Yes," he finally decided. "I want you to keep an eye on both of them. Mrs. Valiant and Neutrino. We need to keep this thing under control."

Stoan didn't notice the slight start Mimik gave when he said, "this thing," which implied a behavior that had been noticed previously.

"I'll check in if there's anything further to report."

"Thank you, Mimik. Very good. That will do."

# 6

Wiley added to the general confusion of the day by wisely insisting that all operations improving Aldierra must be documented via a variety of viewpoints. His people – and Dr. Mem-Bazer did indeed have loyal squadrons of "people" located throughout the AffSys – arranged for and helped prepare such. He had a list of acceptable historians and approaches he wanted to use and messaged the Starharts in triplicate to that effect.

Wiley would provide the financing and ships to ferry everyone to Aldierra. As a leading Legionnaire, his theoretical pockets were just as deep as those of Londo and Jae.

"Do we need to get guards for the female documentarians?" Lina asked her husbands as they read the memo.

"Guards for everyone," Jae said.

Aldierra was a dangerous place.

Despite the hectic schedule, the three Starharts had endeavored to have one meal a day alone together or at least apart from others, one that began with them making their individual journal entries. Wiley called them to complain if they didn't record them. Which he'd had to do several times already. History would want this record, he insisted. Linking the journal making with their shared meal forced them to remember the duty. The quicker they got it over with, the quicker they could relax and enjoy each other.

On this day they did their entries before lunch, which allowed the Tour's "afternoon" participants a little more time to arrive. The Tour's projected route started with several days at Deseed, then hopped along the perimeter of the Affiliated Systems to allow for easier travel for those needing to take the course. Still some delegations would have problems arriving in time for the final session. Even with hyperspace ships, distances across the galactic sector could be vast. Too many worlds desperately needed to learn Lina's technique.

Lina had begun journaling by utilizing the trick of tapping her earring three times at pertinent points in her day, which bookmarked the 24/7 recording the device in it made. Someday soon she'd go back and put it all together, but things were too busy now.

Just before lunch every day she hurriedly checked what she'd noted and chose the most important points. She took about eight minutes to make her base day's report and hoped that would be enough for Wiley for now. Though he was likely checking out her bookmarks as well. Maybe she could get him to include them all in her journal. Maybe there was a way to automate the process.

Time to figure all that out once the Tour was over.


Jae scheduled their next visit to Aldierra that "evening" before final dinner. He aimed Lina's port at a central telecommunications point run by the Aldierran military. She, like her husbands, had a script on her padd. She'd managed to practice it only three times. Jae had roughed it in and Londo did the refining. He was known for giving exceptional speeches, but today they needed only plain talk.

"We'll have to have our own before long," Londo grumbled of the telecommunications setup as they waited for the lights in the main studio to be adjusted. "Our own everything. There's too much chance things might be censored or edited by an outside agency like this."

"Ca-ching," Lina whispered back.

Jae had warned them that the military still wasn't acting nearly fast or far enough. It was up to the three of them to step in, create some momentum.

Lon wondered aloud if they'd be "momentuming" all the way until Doomsday.

"We'll put on our boots and wade in," Lina declared, though she was the only one of the three who didn't own such footwear. They were all promising so much, but even Jae and Lon's fabled resources, which she was going to look into very soon, as in two minutes after the Tour ended, could stretch only so far.

Lina slowly turned in a circle to take in the rather stinky facility. At some point she must get out and actually see this world. Until then she'd have to be satisfied with being indoors on Aldierra and getting the feel of things from an artificial environment.

Despite the technology, the room seemed like a normal broadcast studio: a place in front of cameras for people to perform, then the cameras, which here were long, horizontal strips of curved midair rainbow light, and the control room behind it all, where real humans worked with computers to format and broadcast. Various holograms floated about within all three areas; for what reasons, she had no idea. Most were obscure symbols or moving graphics.

She swore to herself that somehow she'd come up with extra money so she could hire a tutor to explain this tech. She was tired of feeling like an idiot. The Speaker for the Three Worlds couldn't afford to be one.

"I need to talk with women," she mentioned to her husbands. "A sample from all social classes, different locations. Can you get me some?" Man, it sounded like she was ordering groceries.

"I'll add it to the list," Jae told her and nodded to the director, who had appeared in hologram form to point at them. Three odd symbols appeared around his head, changing colors.

This much she'd learned: It was showtime.

"Thirty seconds."

Lina stiffened at the sound of that voice. Granger!

"Please take your positions."

She fought for breath, for movement. The voice wasn't Granger's. It was the director.

Not. Granger.

Her inhale was a long, deliberate one. The exhale was shaky.

**Let's schedule you for a therapist,** Londo told her silently. **Tonight.**

**Not now.** Next two breaths were better. Good. Lina shook the fear from her shoulders.

They'd agreed that the Speaker would go first, since when Aldierra had channeled directly through her, Lina's image had appeared to every Aldierran alive. Lina put a friendly expression on her face, hoping it masked the anxiety that, frankly, was getting to be old hat. Next to the memory of Granger, it was almost a pleasant sensation.

"Hello to all Aldierra. I'm talking men and women alike, adults and children. I am Lina Starhart, and we are the emissaries of the Three Worlds." She introduced her husbands as her husbands (Lon had put up a fuss at that idea, but Jae and she had reminded him that polygamous marriages were the norm on this planet) (likely because of the lack of women) and gave their official Three Worlds titles as well as cape names. The recording of their Initiation would be available to all for streaming.

Then they got down to business. They took turns explaining that people shouldn't panic just because the threat of planet-wide doom had been given to them. If things went well, if people cooperated and did their best, nine months would see them not only saved but living under better conditions with even better ones coming.

They explained that even with the military's assistance, the three of them wouldn't be able to handle everything at the same time. Work would begin at points on all five Aldierran continents but they needed help to settle on a firm approach. They were going to tackle the worst projects first in the manner of triage as well as cause-and-effect. This would mean enlisting a lot of Aldierrans to help them, most being volunteers. Also, people were expected to begin their own local projects without the three of them spearheading things.

Londo looked straight into the camera with his famous – possibly even here, where previously they'd only known him by far-off reputation – frown to lay down the law. "We are three people. We have powers, but still are only three. The primary people who will get this job done…" Here the director's symbols changed, and Lina knew from their discussions that somehow everyone's TV set was being turned into a mirror. "…Are you. You are responsible for saving your own world."

Jae added. "There are twenty billion of you. Even if every single person only takes one small step each day, imagine the progress that can be made. You all can do that even as we begin changing your attitudes, which will anchor your path to a better future. I'll be talking with you about that in the days to come."

"We will make specific goals," Lon said. "We will have points along the way where we can declare that such-and-such step is done, and we can move on from there."

"This campaign will be as transparent as possible," Lina said. "If you see that we're doing something wrong because we're strangers here and don't necessarily have all the answers, speak up. For heaven's sake, speak up quickly! We have a rudimentary communications network in operation right now and we're working to make that better. We want to hear from everyone who needs to be heard from. We want you to stop us if we're making a mistake. We want to hear your ideas, whether they be global or local.

"We want to celebrate the heritage and culture of your localities. We want to make as much of this work as fun as we possibly can. We want people reaching out to help others because you are all of this world, all of one family."

Their first major projects would be cleaning water and air, providing safe habitats for both flora and fauna, redesigning cities as needed… and assisting the state of women of the world.

"Women are people too." Lina tried to drive that point home. "They are not here just for men to use or bully, enslave or hide."

Jae spoke of the physically and mentally handicapped, of the mentally ill. The people who needed help should be sorted out so aid could get to them. They'd be setting up health programs that would expand on existing ones by providing AI like what the AffSys used. "Plus, we hope to import medical personnel from other worlds."

"The AffSys is sending food," Londo added. "The first shipments should arrive in three or four days. I've requested distribution channels to be ready to supply the most desperate. Be patient and we can get everyone seen to. Speaking of patience…"

The frown reappeared. "Everyone has to learn to control their anger. From this moment forward, there will be zero tolerance on acts of violence. That includes all forms of police; law enforcement that is too harsh will be dealt with swiftly. We're not sure yet what punishments will be, but they will be suitable to the circumstances. Violence can tilt the balance. Your world is awaiting judgment. Just don't do violence and you won't have to worry about the consequences."

"Be kind to one another," Lina begged the people.

And so it went.


A timed stim woke up Lina the next morning. Ooh, there was someone behind her in bed. His arm lay upon her own.

Carefully she lifted that arm and rolled over to find Londo spread out across the bed, face-up, his arms flung out as far as they could reach. This seemed to be his favored sleeping position.

She leaned to whisper in his wonderful ear. "Lon, love. Darling." Lightly she stroked the length of his nearest arm.

No response.

Louder. "Lon." She squeezed that arm.

He made a sound that wasn't quite coherent, just a syllable, and retreated further into sleep.

Darn it, it had been a long time. They were newlyweds. She was awake. She poked his shoulder, none too gently. "Londo!"

"Uhh. Jabba no badda," Londo mumbled, or something close to that. He rolled away from her. A slight snore then emitted from him.

Lina said a rather rude word before she dragged herself out of the warm bed, away from its so-hunky inhabitant. She then slogged her way through a quick shower, made a note to do some kind of journal entry at breakfast because she just remembered some stuff from the previous day, and set out to find a real stim – maybe two – and some food before the morning class.

Her day's schedule, which she read once she was out in the hallway, a Legion guard trailing her, told her that Jae had once again altered things beginning at lunch; however, the morning class would proceed on time right after they changed worlds. She didn't have to rush, darn it.

Last night Lina had hardly noticed Londo when she got back to the room. He'd been as awake then as she was now, had even coordinated his Legion schedule to be there, but her stims had been running out and the world was faintly double-imaged. Lon had tried to start something but she'd fallen asleep on him almost immediately.

She should apologize when next she saw him. He'd understand about the stims, wouldn't he? The puter clearly showed her that he'd scheduled a good nap yesterday. She hadn't been able to do that. Jae had also had one.

That was yet another thing she needed to check into: coordinating sleep schedules, with "sleep" in quotation marks. She noted it on her padd with underlines and exclamation marks. "Sleep" was important, dammit.

A steady diet of stims absolutely required both exercise and healthy eating. This hotel didn't have a gym or anything she recognized as a gym – what, you put on a full-body suit that periodically squished you all over? Or sat in a vibrating chair? What kind of exercise was that? – but somebody somewhere had done some research, made a deal, and as of yesterday there was some basic equipment set up in the secured dining room.

The three treadmills of the collection actually resembled true treadmills. If you wanted to, you could run through holographic countrysides instead of watching them on a screen. Lina set hers to silent mode so she could talk with her assistants and hear outside the illusion, while still enjoying a picturesque tour of otherworldly terrain. Lina had chosen a path that ran beside a river that interrupted a plain of gently waving grains. The sky was ever so slightly golden with a weird horizon glow and a sun a bit on the bluish side.

The others used them too, and even more equipment joined the treadmills today so everyone who wanted (and Lina made sure everyone did; sometimes she had to rely on "Bitch Lina" to get things done) assembled so they could have a team meeting and get their muscles taken care of at the same time.

Today she didn't have to inhale her breakfast and could meditate for twenty blessed minutes afterward. The Tour's primary doctor, Mart, came by to discuss her wakeup time the next morning, and gave her and the others appropriately timed stims that would hit now and then throughout the day.

Some of the assistants were more tired than others and Mart dutifully attended to them. Yes, it was exhausting work, but Lina loved helping people and the more zombies she saw, the more anxious participants representing anxious worlds who rushed in to begin class, the more she knew that what she was teaching was badly needed.

It was her joy to help.

Thank goodness they had those stims.

# 7

This particular morning, she needed an extra stim so she could port everyone to their next stop, the planet called Richie, or that's what it sounded like. They'd been on Deseed for three full days. The last of the Tour would be one-day affairs, changing worlds each day. She saw to the porting of twenty-three people, plus a few Legionnaires and whatnot, including Londo who'd finally managed to get out of bed, and those people's baggage. After the first three handfuls the seemingly effortless power of porting felt to Lina like she'd been digging a ditch. Was her body really that tired? Thus the extra early stim.

Its effects made her hop in place, eager for the new day's events.

Everyone and everything else were taking the slow way via hyperspace. Most Legionnaires had gone on in advance to make sure the situation was secure before the Tour staff et al arrived. The ones who hadn't would clean up on Deseed, then take off for the day-after's destination so they'd be the first ones in.

The Tour no longer had access to Deseed's Mind Controlled. Tishan's hyperspace internment vessels would now be shipping in zombies. There were more than enough to go around. Lina shivered at the thought that Mind Control was so widespread in the galaxy, and had been for centuries. What kind of person would actually take over another's will?

The universe held maniacs far crueler than she'd thought possible. Sure, Dad had treated her worse than an animal sometimes, but he'd only actually tried to kill her the once. Well, maybe twice, if what Dr. Gorgeon said was true.

Emperor Yanist-Glory had kidnapped an innocent little boy and held him for years, torturing and experimenting on him. Poor Londo. The adult Lon had enemies who struck at him every way they could, from direct physical attacks like the ones she'd been caught in, to overpowered psychopaths like Granger, who tried to demonstrate his so-called superiority by wreaking havoc without compunction. He'd destroyed, he'd raped, he'd plotted. Thankfully, he'd been stopped.

Imagine all the victims of Granger, of the emperor. Of the galaxy's many Mind Controllers.

Lina wasn't a violent person, but more and more in this past month she'd thought that solid punches to the jaw were what most of these tormentors needed. She could pity them for their sickness once they'd taken efforts to cure themselves, not before.

She resolved to play this smarter. She was going to get far out of the way when people went after Lon. Or Jae too, she supposed. Both could handle themselves when needed. And both seemed to attract this horrible, perverted type of people to test their limits.

Lina heaved a heavy sigh as she unpacked suitcases in the new hotel room. At least this Tour was cleaning up some of the mess the fiends made. That was something. Something she and everyone involved could be proud of.

Londo had zipped off for Legion duty on this new world after giving her just a peck on the cheek. She still had a few minutes before she had to report for the day's classes. Lon hadn't unpacked yet so she opened his duffel and tried to guess where he might want things. Oh my, men's underwear. And what were these objects? Boxes and flat things and some kind of wearable straps…

Jae's bags had been put in his room – they had to get him a separate room to maintain the facade – and she wondered if he'd unpacked yet.

She turned to find her Feithi husband behind her. Jae caught her in an embrace and satisfying kiss on the mouth, where kisses belonged, and ran his thumb over her cheek. "Are you getting enough stims?" he asked her as he examined her face. "Enough sleep? Exercise? And water. Excessive stims dehydrate you. I looked it up."

Ooh, Jae. Wonderful Jae. This was more like it. "I'm working on it. You're looking great. As usual. Someone scheduled a recovery day after this, didn't they? What day is this?"

He gave her a rocking hug. "Four. Deseed, Richie, Traim, and Sute. Only two more days to go. The press is clamoring to hear from you."

There was something else going on. She could feel a particularly sore spot on Jae's back; see a faded bruise across his jaw. His eyes held tension. "How are things out there?" she asked.

He shrugged.

"Don't pull a Londo on me. Tell me the truth. Something's happening. I can feel it. I'm getting the anxiety. I hear swords clanging, of all things. You're not using swords?" Her guides sometimes fed her the darnedest symbols!

That made his lips twitch. "Far from it. We all have our powers as well as cutting-edge weaponry to work with. There's some trouble out there, but that's what we're for: to protect the Tour. Don't worry about it."

"Well… Okay." The Legion had the biggest reputation around. They could handle anything, it seemed.

"Every world for three sectors is scrambling to get delegates to attend your seminars." Jae noted her anxious expression and said, "Don't worry about that either. I'll handle the press as well."

"Thanks, honey. I really appreciate it." He was so warm. He'd been warm in bed yesterday morning, too. Lina had taken a few precious minutes to watch him sleep. He didn't snore at all, while Londo sometimes snored just a little that Lina had noticed so far, kind of a periodic wheeze. Jae's hair hung down in his face when he slept on his side, and she'd brushed it back so she could gaze at his sweet features. He was certainly the most beautiful person she'd ever seen. He slept in the nude and Londo slept in his underwear most nights.

Neither choice was to Legion regs.

Was this usual for them, or were they also adapting to their unusual situation? When would life switch gears to an easier pace so they could really begin to learn about each other? When would they have time to immerse themselves in lovely lust? Would they ever have a honeymoon, or would they jump past that emotional phase of marriage? More and more Lina was beginning to realize the importance of that phase, but it was difficult to be horny when a stim dictated your state of consciousness. Still, that urge lurked underneath it all.

Especially when Jae had his arms around her.

"You call Londo 'honey.'" Jae murmured against her.

"Can't I call you that, too?" She stood on tiptoe so she could kiss the line of his lovely jaw.

"I want a pet name all my own. I don't want you confusing us."

"Jae, honey…" Lina withdrew so she could study his expression. "Oh, sorry. No, I'm not. Jae, honey, I hardly know you yet. I do know that I never mix the two of you up. After the Tour is over, we'll have time. 'Honey' is a catch-all for everyone who's precious to me. It's not a pet name."

He leaned down to touch his forehead to hers and her breath caught. She could feel his heartbeat under her hand. "I want you," he said and pulled her back to him.

Oh yes. Her mind reached out to his and they wrapped themselves around each other. Through each other.

Beyond his maleness and drive, he was starlight. He was a direct connection to higher, brighter states of consciousness and all the power, joy, and knowledge that held – though he blocked off most of it. The catastrophic trauma Jae had endured as a child when the rest of his world died had–

"And you are life. You are a growing, a learning, a link to all others," he whispered to her.

Yes, this was mind sharing. The love pulsed back and forth between them. But her body reacted to his, both crackling with need. Hunger and heat. Deep-down animal urges. It was so very…

Dammit!

"Jae, this is not a good time–"

He caught her with a long kiss. Lust washed over the spiritual link like a wave of magma, sparking her every nerve fiber, and Lina fought herself to push away.

"I'm sorry," she said. "Jae, I love you. I want you so much too, and I want to know you and talk with you and make love with you for days and days. But class–"

"Class." Jae frowned at her and then sighed. "But. I'm frustrated. I mean, we just got married and we haven't even–"

Lina shook her head. "Me too. And no, we haven't, have we? Not since our vows, us two together." A slow smile came to her as she began to imagine what it would be like, just she and Jae together, now that they were married. Now that they knew they loved each other.

"Yeah," he breathed. "That's what I want."

"I promise. But–"

"But."

"Yeah. You and Londo can still – I mean, I'm dead to the world when I conk out," she told him.

"So we noticed. We've taken advantage of that." That elfin grin lit his face devilishly. "We've taken advantage of that a lot. We clear you off the bed, but we do so very carefully. And afterward we tuck you back in."

She let out a soft howl of frustration. "Lucky Londo. Lucky Jae."

That brought a chuckle from him. "I'm sorry. Once we get off the Tour and have Aldierra up and running, we'll take some time off as couples. We'll act like newlyweds. But I tell you, it's wrecking me. Out in public, I can't do anything. Londo says something if I even look at him funny."

"So he's upset by it, too. That's good. That means we can do away with this secrecy thing soon, and good riddance."

"No, it means that we take it at Londo's pace. Don't nag him about this, Lie-Lie. This is all new to him." He shook his head. "When I took the class I wanted to tell everyone, 'That's my Lina up there!' I almost did. Caught myself at the last moment. But we need to keep Lon's needs in mind. We need to be patient."

He moved away and began to sort through Lon's clothing. Dresser drawers opened to his gesture, and he placed underwear in them. Lon's extra suits unrolled wrinkle-free from the luggage.

She shouldn't take even this long, but it was so good just to chat with Jae, and oh my, he was proud of her. "Since when are you patient?" Lina asked just to devil him. "It's new to me, too."

"By choice." He turned to gather more clothing. "He never had one. He was Valiant, too powerful ever to have sex with anyone until you came along to show him how." Jae transferred hangers to his right hand so he could brush a long curl out of her face with his left. "You pointed that out to me, remember? He never truly had to think about his own sexuality, much less consider coming out of the closet. He hasn't begun to gain his footing on this. We've got to give him as much time as he needs."

Lina reached out to him before he could move away. She sagged against his chest. He was so much taller than Londo. And he smelled – she smiled. He smelled of her shampoo.

"It reminds me of you through the day," he whispered to her. "Just keep wearing those awful pajamas."

"Awful? I thought Legion Protocol would approve."

"Awful. And keep getting dressed and undressed in the bathroom, or I'll throw you off your schedule and onto your back."

"My schedule!"

Lina's eyes flew open and she pushed away from Jae. He had to clench the hangers so they wouldn't fall from his hands. Lina grabbed a sealed bottle of water from a table. "What time is it? I'm back to being late. Golly day, I told Wiley I'd give him an update before class, and I'm supposed to check in with the crew and clear myself and get a briefing from Legion Security and–"

"Go." Jae patted her on the bottom and pushed her out the room door. "Hurry!"

"Wait!"

She ran back inside the room, closing the door behind her. She reached up to Jae and gave him as deliberate a kiss as she could manage for a rush job. "You have a good day," she told him firmly. "Stay safe. I love you. I don't ever want us to leave each other without saying that."

"I love you." He gave her a special smile that she'd never seen before. She liked it. He kissed her again and then she left.

Lina and her assistants made more adjustments to the class structure as they progressed, adding minor techniques and explanations to it. Now everyone was taught how to clean an area of negative energies, utilizing the hoops of light technique that had astonished Chimrin. Lina noticed the Tishan assistants always got a kick out of doing this for they could actually see the hoops whereas she and her friends could only imagine them. She smiled at them, no longer aliens but real persons with their own ways of looking at the world.

She noticed she was slowing down sooner than expected, so at a break she called in Dr. Mart. Ordinarily he was on staff under Dr. Riz Gorgeon at Legion HQ but had been assigned to the Tour along with some other medical staffers. He always seemed to be the one ready whenever one of the assistants needed help. Lina wondered if he were taking stims too.

After consulting with Riz about the staff's fatigue, Mart gave the group twice the normal amount of timed stims to keep them in top form. Good thing stims weren't addictive and could be used in large amounts for a limited time.

It worked out to far more than fourteen hours' work a day for Lina, hours more than the others had to put in. Their days had to be much longer than those of the world they were on. She wondered how many real days their six-day tour was taking, and then shrugged to herself. It would take what it took. She hoped Mart had packed enough stims.

During one class break Lina actually took her own advice and asked her guides how they thought things were going. They motioned to her side and she looked there, expecting – what? The only thing that was there was...

She reached, and the magical flute the Three Worlds had given her as a gift at her Investiture melted into view. She took a moment to admire the golden instrument that was covered with lovely leaflike designs. If she truly studied it, she thought she saw tiny, half-hidden fairy faces in the foliage smiling at her. Producing the flute pleased her guides, so she lifted it to her lips and played "Simple Gifts," then ran through the verse once again as she felt her own spirits rise.

The music invigorated her, or perhaps it was just the flute. It was wondrous. Only she and Jae and Lon could touch it, as she could touch the gifts they'd been given. She loved playing it, or perhaps that was the emotion it gifted her. Its music communicated the mood of the piece she played. "Simple Gifts" made her feel as if Mart had just given her a stim as wakefulness. Purpose again flooded her system. She felt more connected to the universe.

**What was that?** Jae called to her from outside and she explained.

**We felt that throughout the hotel,** he told her. **Everyone liked it. Good to know we have this available.**

Lon may have his amazing new shield and Jae his staff of authority, but she had her flute. That had been gifted to her. It was with a little jaunt in her step that she finished the class.

Though people began to leave after the day's second session, some came up to the stage with further questions. One of Lina's Tishan assistants reported to her about the results of the variations he had tried using a Tishana slant. Unfortunately, it seemed that the original technique was the more efficient one and he was a bit chagrined to admit it. She patted his arm sympathetically. It was worth a test.

"Excuse me a minute," Lina said and ported back to her empty room. Her darned surgical tape had slipped. She got out the roll from her supplies and attached more strips to the palm-sized Ruby she had fastened to her chest inside her bra. At first it had chafed but by now she was comfortable with the weight of it, the shape of it there next to her heart and her Three Worlds tattoo.

It was the Ruby of power she'd taken from Paul Granger, the man who had tried to rape her. The man who *had* raped and beaten Demi – Olympia – to within a millimeter of her life. Granger was still in a Washington, DC ICU and wouldn't be able to be moved for some time, but as soon as he could, she was going to port him to Aum at the center of the galaxy and tell those Galactic Sentinel bosses of his a few things. The Ruby would go as well. Maybe they could find a nice new owner for it.

Her breath caught before she could snuggle it more firmly into place with her fingers. *No, no, no.* She tried to breathe. Terror froze her muscles.

The scenes of that night returned: Granger bending over her, grinning at what he was going to do. Boasting about his power over her… and by extension, Londo. He hated Lon. Lina was merely an object to be used for his vengeance.

And later… She'd been held helpless by the power of this Ruby, directed by Granger. Forced to watch Granger pummel Demi until she was senseless. Lina's heart pounded at the vivid vision, imprinted into her soul. Demi, the legendary Olympia. The hero of a thousand crises. Then he'd used this Ruby to augment himself as he raped her, plunged into her and ripped her open. There had been nothing Lina could do except plead with the Ruby to stop aiding its master.

"Not your fault," Lina murmured to the Ruby as the pads of her fingers met it. "Not your fault. I don't know what those people do to you to make you obey your Galactic Guard masters, but you stood up to him. You knew what was right, and you did it."

She caressed the Ruby like a pet. The action seemed to calm her as well. "You were wonderful. Inspiring. But it must have taken so much out of you to go against your training. How many centuries have you worked for the Brigade? Maybe millennia. But you rose to the occasion."

Imagine: the Ruby funneled unimaginable power from the black hole at the center of the Milky Way. In the wrong hands it had turned into a deadly weapon. Its basic integrity had allowed it to turn its back on its master. If it weren't for this Ruby, Lina and Demi wouldn't be alive. How much must that have cost it?

With that she let out a breath of release. "I'm so proud of you. The Galactic Sentinels will be too, once they hear your story. But for now, you just rest. We'll keep you safe. Just tell me if you need to recharge again, or if you need to lie in sunlight or whatever. I'll do it and make sure you're safe while you do what you need to. Thank you. Thank you for saving me, for saving us.

"You feeling all right now?" Lina asked the Ruby as she secured the final length of tape across it. Its glow increased a moment, and she patted it. "Good. We'll get you some kind of psychological help. I'm not sure how that will work, but we'll try. All of us want you to get well. I want you to be happy." It gave another pulse and she smiled before returning to the class.

# 8

Only her assistants, Londo, and Jae remained in the lecture hall, plus a Legionnaire or two lingering near the exits. Time for dinner. Hotel employees showed them all to a private dining room for the Tour's staff, past a few Legion guards.

There Lina took a steadying breath and then ported in her new father-in-law from Earth. He showed up in shirtsleeves and jeans instead of his celebrated lightning-emblazoned costume. Every assistant froze where they were: standing, seated, or in between. Even the few attending Legionnaires were gaping.

"I heard we weren't supposed to dress up for this," Maximus said, his bass voice filling the room as he took in his new surroundings. A large red padded cube container hung from his Mr. Universe-sized shoulder, and he carried a duffel as luggage.

"*Ça va,* Hal. Whatdya bring?" Londo helped his adoptive father with the baggage. "Is that what I think it is?"

"I thought someone around here might be wanting a little home cooking along about now," Hal said with a grin. "I got the impression it was supper time?"

Lon peered into the big container without opening it. "Hah!" was all he said.

His arms free, Hal reached over to give Jae a noogie. "Rello, Shaggy!" he greeted as the long-haired Legionnaire grimaced and ducked.

"*Why* must you always do that?"

"Because it's fun. Get a haircut, hippie."

Londo and Hal quickly pushed several of the larger tables together. Hesitantly, the assistants moved closer to the legend of legends. The opened container revealed its contents by aroma before the first box was even produced.

"Pizza!" the entire Terran delegation exclaimed as one.

Hal announced, "I got pepperoni. I got sausage. I got cheese. I got meats. I got chicken with some kind of white sauce. I got sausage and pepperoni, extra green pepper and onion."

"That one's his," Lon informed them.

"I got gluten-free. I got two everything-vegetarian minus the pineapple. Hope that's enough to handle everyone."

There was no question about ogling the galaxy's most famous megahero. The pizza had priority. The Terrans dug into it, only pausing to show the Tishana how to handle the treat. Lina made sure Jae had a pack of red pepper flakes. He'd liked those when he'd had pizza before. She gave the same to Londo, though she wasn't sure of his pizza choices.

"Let's get some beer in here," Jae declared, and ordered it through the hotel's system.

"Thanks, Hal," Londo said. "Thanks a bunch. It's just what we needed." Unconsciously they settled into a family grouping at the end of the table: Hal, Lon, Lina, and Jae.

"How are the cats?" Lina asked as she picked black olives off a slice.

Hal nodded. "Maria's got her grand-kits there at Starhaven. They're running them ragged."

"The kids or the cats?" Lon asked, which made Hal laugh.

"Don't worry; they're not bothering the old cat. What's her name?"

"Fafhrd," Lina said. She missed her seven cats. She felt guilty for not thinking about them more often.

"Right. She sleeps a lot, but they're making sure she gets her meds. Now, how's it going here?" Hal asked and Londo and he chatted like they hadn't seen each other in years.

Lina made yakky motions to Jae behind Lon's back and Jae choked on his beer. Then he pointed at Lon. "Don't pick at that!"

Lon stopped twitching his new earring.

"All the time, picking at it," Jae accused.

"It's okay to roll it around a few times a day to keep the hole open," Lina told Londo. "I think."

"But don't pick at it!" Jae warned.

Hal sat with a slice of half-eaten pizza in his hand, his jaw hanging open. "Earring?" he finally managed to say. "It's… pierced. How…? How…?"

Londo jutted his chin in accusation at his two spouses. "Them." His face began to work in the odd, expectant permutations he had made the day before the Tour began, as the earring had been punched into his ear. *Slowly* punched into his ear.

"Wait," Hal said. "First, a tattoo." He pointed at the back of Lon's right hand, which displayed his Three Worlds tattoo, a faint metallic gold against his light brown skin. His gaze flicked to Jae's forehead, which held a matching tat. "Now a piercing?"

"We think it'll be permanent," Jae said, considering said ear.

"We keep telling the cells they're doing a great job," Lina said. "They're committed to keeping the hole open."

"Probably. But if you keep pulling at the damn thing, Lon, they might change their minds," Jae growled.

Lon dropped his hand. "Wiley's got all kinds of recording and communications devices in the earrings," he gave as an excuse, though he liked the different look. It signaled a new phase of his life. He would have taken the earring even it if weren't super-tech. Jae had converted a number of various styles into impervion so they could stand up to the action he saw on a regular basis.

To keep his hands away from the jewelry, Lon showed the larger group an interstellar press conference that Jae had given that morning. They watched, spellbound, as for the first time some of them truly realized the scope of what they were doing. Hal nodded and gazed at his son, then turned to Lina and gave her a proud grin.

"You're looking a little worn out," he told her and turned to the group. "You're all looking tired. Aren't you getting enough sleep?"

"It's not that bad," Dinah blurted as she got up enough courage to address Maximus himself. The others echoed her. "It's just been a long day. They're giving us stims." She sighed. "Ten years ago I could have done this without any stims, no prob."

Lina tore off a final bit of veggie pizza and inhaled the wonderful odors before she ate it. Food Out Here was colorful but textureless, usually presented in scoops. Sometimes it tasted good but mostly it just sat inoffensively on the tongue. "To think, I almost decided to skip supper so I could sneak in an extra hour's sleep tonight. Thank you, Hal. This is really great. No, Jae! You don't put mustard on pizza! Where'd that come from?"

Londo reached around her to snatch the packet from Jae's hands.

"Here now, what's this?"

Dr. Mart walked up to the table, his hand-sensors out. He was on the youngish side of middle age and had a friendly face as well as familiar Terran-style medium brown skin. "I thought I told you people to watch your nutrition."

"I'm sorry." Hal's contriteness was genuine. "I brought in food from home. I didn't know they weren't–"

"It was our responsibility," Lina said. "Sorry, Doc. We forgot. How about fruit for dessert? Can we take vitamins? Run around the block to work it off?"

"No one runs around the block," Londo said quickly. It was the way he said it that made everyone turn to look at him. He shook his head at them, trying to counter the threat his voice had implied. "Just... No one runs around the block. No one goes outside the hotel complex. Not even with a guard."

"Is there something going on out there?" Lina's psychic teacher, Sue, asked. "My guides have been jittery lately. Real jittery. Dinah and I were talking about it."

As if on cue, the Tishana gathered close.

"All I'm saying," Londo told the group, "is that everyone should be aware of following security precautions. If there's any threat, it's outside, not inside. No one's getting in here who hasn't been run three ways through security. We've got everyone booked for inner rooms. Stay away from windows and skylights you might run across, from any outer corridors. After this is over, we'll take the Terrans – and the Tishana, if they're interested – on a short vacation on Sarastor so you can see the sights."

"Lots of sights to see on Sarastor," Jae put in helpfully.

"What's going on, Lon?" Lina quietly asked. "We have a right to know."

"The Legion's handling it," he said.

Lina stuck out her lower lip. Londo had promised he wouldn't lie to her, at least not about the big stuff. But zero information–

"There's been an increase of Mind Control reports," Jae said. "We've got people stationed on the next world out, and they're monitoring there as well – a buildup of Controlled personnel. But we've instituted corridors around this hotel and the next with telepathic dampers. There'll be no Controlling within them. Anything outside –" he shrugged – "we can deal with."

"How much have you been dealing with?" Lina asked.

Again Jae shrugged.

"We are the Legion," Londo said.

"You need help?" Hal asked.

Londo bit back his first reply and then said, "Check in with Stoan or Andri. I think we can handle it ourselves, but you see what they think, too."

Hal nodded.

Subcommander Andri let Maximus take one shift with the Legion and then sent him to quarters to rest until the morning session, which he'd signed up for. He would be taking preliminary notes for Earth's ParaNet, which he led. Those members would get follow-up training at some future date when Lina had spare time.

Hal had attended the first class on the day's new world of Traim. Lina made a mental note that in the future when he was available, she'd encourage him to walk in front of her in crowded areas. People drew back from him in sheer awe of the power he exuded, which created a handy, clear path behind him.

She couldn't chicken out like she had when Jae had attended class, to let others tend to him while she tried not to be dazzled and distracted by his presence. Instead, she was the one to lead Maximus through the exercises. And because the others quakingly refused to. They were still petrified of him.

Hal had watched her instruct Lon and Chimrin back on Earth a week before, so he had a rough idea of what to expect. He tackled the class with the enthusiasm of a child learning something entirely new for the first time. Before long the two of them were laughing as they worked together. Lina would correct his technique and he'd make horrible dad-jokes. "I feel like I should have my rod and reel," Hal told her as he searched for hooks. "All this hoodoo seems fishy to me." "Those folks act like they wouldn't be cod dead humming." "I've haddock with these shenanigans!"

The zombie assigned to him almost passed out four times from adulation alone. Mart had to be called in to make sure the zombie's blood pressure didn't go off the charts. But it didn't. Hal cured the zombie ("Carp-e diem!" he declared with the final swipe), and the man practically pledged his everlasting allegiance to Maximus.

Hal was still laughing as Lina ported him back to Earth.


After class Londo went to get them food while Jae safety-checked their quarters so they could eat there in privacy for once. Here on Traim, Londo and Lina had the presidential suite: a few bedrooms plus a luxurious living room, offices, and a spacious garden room filled with a jungle of indoor plants.

"I don't think she noticed anything but the bed," Jae told Lon when he arrived.

He and Lon made their journal entries and then ate around the living room's entertainment console table, where they could eat with their feet propped up. Lon pressed Jae to eat a little more than he wanted to keep his energy level high.

"Yes, Mother," Jae said with a smile.

"I'll hand-feed you if I have to," Lon tried to put a growl in his voice and failed.

"I'd like to see you try. Here," Jae reached for some energy carbs and stuffed them into a small pack that he hung from his belt. "I'll go through these as needed. All right?"

"*D'accord.*"

"Good. There are better things to do with an extra minute or two." Jae grabbed Londo by the shirt and pulled him to him, both falling back onto the couch.

Lon was chuckling into Jae's shoulder when they heard the wakeup alarm go off in the bedroom, and then the shower start up. Lon reported that Lina was journaling from there. She emerged a while later looking considerably better.

"I just feel so slimy from all the energies anymore," she said as she watched her husbands finish dressing. "I think I'll start playing flute at every break." She squinted at them. "Do I know you? You both look vaguely familiar. Any questions from Aldierra? How are they taking things today?" She sat to take care of the tray of food left for her, still hot and fresh within its stasis cover.

"No news I trust," Jae said. He glanced at Londo. "We need to get those satellites talking to us."

"I'll do that today. Can you port me over before class?" Lon asked Lina.

She stretched her neck and back. "Yeah. Stim just kicked in a few minutes ago. Right as the alarm rang. Mart's got these things timed to a T."

Lon made a sour face. "I don't like that you're on stims so much." He changed his expression to a grimace and before she could reply, said, "Can't be helped."

"No. I just thank goodness they're available. It's only for the duration," Lina added. "It's not like we're going to be hooked on them. I don't think they're addictive, anyway. We're almost done with the Tour; we'll make it."

Jae nodded. "Tomorrow when I go to Aldierra, I want to talk with some normal people in person, see what's really going on down on the ground," Jae said. He cocked his head at Lina. "But not if I have to stay a few days because you're too exhausted to port me back. Give me a heads-up on your stims schedule."

"You're off to Aldierra? I thought your schedule said—"

Lon and Jae looked at each other. "That's something we've been meaning to talk with you about," Jae said as both focused again on their wife.

"Uh oh."

"They want more classes," Londo told her.

"They what?"

"Look, Lie, there's a waiting list a mile long for this. People are coming from so far away that even though they left days ago when we first announced, they're still in transit. The entire sector's begging for this."

"And you were going to tell us this when?"

Jae touched her arm. "We're going to sit everyone down after class tonight and lay things out for them. We figure an extra three days. Three days, right?"

"Maximum," Londo confirmed with a determined nod. "Tell your people there's going to be a demand for more seminars in the future, but they don't have to happen right now. Nine days on this is our absolute max. We have more important things to do."

"Plus we have the recordings. We'll make lots of copies."

"How does this affect Aldierra?" Lina asked weakly.

"Bracken says that they'd welcome three more days to organize. Maybe four. I'll give them a kick." Lina thought Jae used the word in the English way, a violent verb, instead of as the Sarastoran expletive. "Lon and I want to contact more non-military people, get them moving on some of our projects. We have some names now."

"You need to have a full day to recover from this, kitten, plus a rest day. We start on Aldierra in six days."

"Me in six days. All of us in six days." Lina could picture herself having survived long, long hours. There was another side to this, a light at the end of a tunnel. "These stims had better be extra good," she concluded.

"You said you were going to play the flute more. Play it a lot."

Lina said slowly, "I can't believe I'm saying this. What if we added another class for these last days? Piled on the stims?"

Her husbands looked at each other.

"I'll ask Mart," Jae decided.

Lon rubbed his nose. "If we do that… We camp out here for an extra day. You won't have to port everyone tomorrow. Much less work. Final three days on one world as well."

Jae checked his padd. "That would be Sute."

"I don't know. It makes sense, but I may be caffeine-deprived. Won't that affect–"

Jae was consulting his padd. "There are already tens of extra delegations headed this way, or even arrived by now. The next venue's only a few hyperspace hours away. Easy enough for all to reach in time even if they arrive here first. Three days, yes. That'll work. In the meantime, Lie, no caffeine for you," Jae ordered. "Not even your tea. I think it'll interfere with the stims. I'll talk with Mart to confirm."

Lina stuck her tongue out at him.

Lon rubbed her shoulders. "We'll talk after this class, kitten. To everyone. Jae will have alternatives worked out with Stoan and Andri by then, right?"

Jae nodded. "Let's get out of here afterward for dinner. I'm getting cabin fever. Someplace with a view even if it's just screens. I've been hearing about this string of moons Traim has..."

"I could live with that," Londo said. "A change for everyone on staff. I'll arrange guards." He touched Lina's cheek. "And you need a solid, no-interruptions meal before bed. I'll talk with Gorgeon to get her input on everything."

Riz Gorgeon, chief of Legion Medical back on Sarastor, was a budding friend. "Yes, Londo," Lina finally said.

Lon smirked. "The two best words in any language. Say it again."

"Yerfullofit, Londo," Lina told him as she gave him a quick kiss and squeezed Jae's hand. "At least that's how I think it's pronounced here."

Jae snorted, but he was also looking at his Legion ring, the central control for his Array. It was useful enough that even Lon wore a ring, though not the rest of the Array. He could hear the report coming in to Jae, but Lina couldn't.

"Gotta go," Jae announced when it ended. He finished fastening his cape to his shoulders, adjusted the wrist and ankle bands that were also a part of his Array, and gave Lon a quick kiss. Then he did the same to Lina, squeezing her shoulder before he trotted off to exit their quarters.

Lina looked dazed. "Too quick," she decided. "I love you."

From beyond the hallway outside came, **I love you too.**

Her face settled into a slight frown. "That's wrong. We say that in person." She turned to Londo. "We say that in person," she insisted. "Do we need to make a notarized rule?"

Lon's mouth twisted. "We'll figure this out soon, at least to start feeling like—"

"Like we're married," Lina finished for him.

He heaved a self-pitying sigh. "*Oui.* Things will straighten out once the Tour's over. We'll all be on the same schedule. We shall have enough sleep and enough food and enough sex," Londo told her.

"I hope I'll be included in that last part. Once I get that sleep," Lina said.

He took some fruit and protein-smeared bread and handed it to her. "Eat some more," he ordered.

"Class," she responded, adjusting her belt as she moved toward the door.

"So eat on the way." He gathered more transportable food and brought it along as he strolled beside her. "What was all that about a Controller showing up the other day? I still haven't heard the full story."

Through her chewing, she related the tale to him as they walked to the auditorium, Londo shaking his head the entire time.

"Next time you get a Legionnaire to deal with it. Right away, no snarking around."

"I did get a Legionnaire. Brügz, whom I believe is a big-wig Legionnaire. Ex-commander, is he not? And that snarking gave us a good lesson. We've rerun it in all the classes since. You'll see it." She patted his hand. "If it looked like it was going to get out of control, I'd have hit the panic button and called in the troops."

Lon ground his teeth but nodded. "This is not the safe life I wanted to give you. None of it has been."

"It'll settle soon, won't it?"

The hall widened out here at the front entrance of the auditorium, but it also offered some shadowy niches. Lon stopped in one and leaned his shoulder against the wall. His jutted his lower lip and moved it side to side thoughtfully. "Define 'settle.'"

"You know. Normal married life."

"I've been thinking, Lie. I don't think I've ever led a 'normal' life. Not since I was three."

Before he'd been kidnapped by aliens who'd incubated powers like Maximus' in him.

"So we'll carve one out."

He raised his eyebrows at her. "Have you noticed who you've married? What you've signed up for? We're not going to be able to relax until this Aldierra thing is over, one way or another. And after that…"

"After that we'll have to expand to Sarastor and Earth," Lina said. She settled back next to him. "I hate what this is doing to the cats. They don't understand."

"We might haul them around with us once the Tour is over. On occasion."

"But cats don't like to change–" Lina sighed in surrender. "We'll figure it out."

He twisted so his body curved around her, his face just above hers. "Do you think it'll be very bad? Your life?"

She gave him a slow smile. "Not as long as you're in it." ***And Jae.***

They murmured about little things they loved about each other there in the shadows, rubbing their hands over arms and shoulders and hips. Kissing only their lips and faces. Caressing with clothing on.

Chim's voice cut through their pleasure. "You're broadcasting, Starharts." She stood there, tapping on her forehead about telepathic exposure. "Learn better control. And too much PDA. Five minutes, Lina. You did want to meditate before class, didn't you? Lon, you're on duty in a few minutes, right?"

***Have you told him?*** Chim asked.

"Who?" Lon asked. Then realization dawned on his face. ***Oh, you mean Hal, about the Triune.*** "No. Not yet."

"Make it soon," his Legion mentor ordered. "You draw this out, the worse it will get."

Lina made a face at her and Chim laughed. "Yes, I do get a kick out of nagging him. Now say goodbye, Londo. There's a class to be taught; a sector to be saved."

Chim was right. Lina made another face, this one of resignation and aimed at Lon. "Guess I gotta go," she said."

"I'll talk with Gorgeon."

"Right. I love you."

He gave her that wonderful Londo smile. "I love you too." Then he gave her a very satisfactory kiss.

# 9

"Three extra days? With extra classes?" Dinah exclaimed as the group gathered after the "afternoon" session. "Can we do it?"

"Should we start tonight?" Lina asked her people.

Lon checked his padd. "We have enough participants and then some," he assured them. "Those who were gathering at the next venue had enough warning to get here. Most of them. Plus a few extras who showed up." He took stock of the group's expressions. "If you don't agree, they can hop in their ships and return to… well, wherever it is we're supposed to go in two days, and still be on time for class."

The Tishana Angha said hesitantly, "Those stims are good. I think we need to up the dosage, though."

"Even so we'll need more down-time," David Autry insisted, and Mar-yo agreed.

Lon faced the assistants, of whom so many had their arms crossed across their chests. "Doctor Gorgeon says you can stand the extra days on stims with no serious aftereffects. We may be able to work in some longer sleep periods."

"They can't start without us," Lina observed. "We'll definitely schedule longer sleep periods if this goes through."

"*D'accord.* If you're interested, I checked with Field Marshal Bracken and he seemed relieved to have the extra time to get things organized on Aldierra, so this helps us there. How about it?"

"Fine with me, I guess," Dinah said. "I mean, I'm really tired, I think I might skip supper–"

"Don't," Londo ordered, and she nodded.

"–But I think I can go the extra days. With the stims. And Lina's flute."

The others agreed, and the schedule was set.

"Two hour break then before the third class today. I'll get someone to adjust the rest periods. Remember," Londo reminded them before he left with his wife, "you eat healthy, you get your rest when you can, you get moderate exercise, and you pay attention to all security protocol. No exceptions. We're doing what we can out there to protect you, but we can't protect you if you do something stupid."

"No sir, Valiant!" "No way!"

"Good."


"New directions," Lon's lieutenant, the giant insectoid Mimik, informed Lina just before the first extra class. Dr. Mart had given the staff their doses of timed stims, so everyone was wide awake. "We'll have two uniformed Legionnaires inside for each session, over and above your class roster, which contains plainclothed Team Leaders. It's just a precaution. And this way we get two more Legionnaires per session in to see this, though the costumes won't be participants."

Lina frowned. Just how much were Lon and Jae telling her and how much were they leaving out? What kind of chaos was going on outside these hotels?

"Just a precaution," Mimik repeated, and Lina nodded.

She checked in with her assistants, quickly walking down the corridor toward the lecture hall. David, who when he wasn't helping worlds free themselves from Mind Control, had a tarot and astrology business back in Durham, trotted up beside her. "I did some souvenir shopping off the internet here during break," he said.

"Oh? Cool, find anything interesting?"

"I was able to access my online accounts. I found out how much they're paying us for this. I was wondering, with the new schedule… You didn't warn us."

"Warn you?" Lina's eyebrows knit together. "You should be getting a nice wage for this. Generous. With overtime and bonus. Lon and Jae told me how much this class is in demand, how people are raving about it. I'll track down someone after class and find out what's going on. We'll see that–"

"No, no." He tried to slow her down. "It's not that at all. One of my security guards showed me how to look it up, and I found American dollar equivalents, or at least that's what he said it was."

"American dollar equivalents?" Lina considered the problem. "Oh, Wiley's Terran studies must have coordinated with–"

"I'm trying to tell you," David said with an exasperated huff. "You say we've got four days left before we're done. I think– now, I may be off by twenty thousand or so– I think that we're all going to go back to Earth as hundred-thousandaires. High hundred-thousandaires."

Lina took a beat to absorb that. "Holy shit," she finally whispered.

"Holy shit is right." David grinned. "Do you realize that I'll finally be able to pay my accountant? And my father's always told me that I should settle down and earn a real living. I can't wait to hear what he has to say about this." He actually giggled as they crossed to the back of the stage.

"Is it true?" Sue Taylor asked, wide-eyed. She looked at David suspiciously. She and David had gone through a rough breakup a year before. "Did he get the figures right?"

"I bet he misplaced the decimal," Dinah accused. Sue was her best friend.

"I'll check after class," Lina promised. "I'll see Lon or Jae then, maybe. Until then, don't get your hopes up. Be pleasantly surprised by whatever they pay us."

"Very pleasantly," David smirked.


Dr. Mart had reluctantly given Lina extra stims after the long third class. Lon and Jae had had the temerity to offer their opinions about the decision. Lon used his darkest scowl at her, the cad, while Jae crossed his arms over his chest, his features a mask of non-emotion. How she hated that one!

"They're strictly timed," the doctor warned her, them, and Erik, aka Sunstorm, who alertly stood with the group in the presidential suite.

"They're just stims." Lina frowned back at her husbands.

Erik and she had gotten to know each other well while Lina had been held under house arrest in Wiley's lab for a week. He had spent duty time there as central command had been temporarily housed in that lab under Wiley's watch. Erik had fearlessly worked on the Rimhold insurrection as well as helping to mop up the invasion of Sarastor. Now Jae instructed him that he was to make sure Lina ported back well before the stim wore off.

"For some reason he doesn't trust me," Lina pouted as soon as they came out of the port.

"That's because Jae's smart," the redheaded Legionnaire replied. He'd ported interstellar a few times before so the period of blankness wasn't nearly as terrifying as it had been the first time.

"You're just trying to endear yourself to your Team Leader. Have you met up with Dinah yet? She was asking about you."

"She was?" Erik's expression of pleased surprise changed and he gave Lina a side-eye. "You playing matchmaker? Dr. Mem-Bazer said Terrans like to do that."

"I am merely reporting on my personnel," Lina replied haughtily.

"Seems to me that you've got enough to do just with the Tour."

"I know that's important, but so are other things. Like this. I need to get more involved with our Aldierran mission," Lina insisted. "This is the most essential item that we still haven't firmed up. It's something I can do.

"Lon's in charge of… Valiant stuff. Bashing and building." She waved her hands in the air. "Boom! Crash! Bam! He's very good at that."

Erik nodded. "A fair description of his technique."

Then she feigned holding a staff while pointing ahead, like Moses in the Wilderness. "Jae's going to be pointing the way and making sure people understand the why and importance of what it is they're going to be doing. He'll make sure what we do blends in with their culture, and is something they can carry on. He'll also pay particular attention to flora and fauna. While I…"

She opened her arms, questioning. "I am Three Worlds coordination. And I have no idea how I'm supposed to do that, other than port people and things around."

"You do that well."

"There are twenty billion people on Aldierra."

He shrugged. "Might take a few stims."

She joined him in his laugh, but it had worn on her: having the military in charge of emergency communications routing. For some reason women were scarce on Aldierra. Jae said they were definitely in an inferior position, though he wasn't sure of the details. They were hidden, likely against their will.

The horror of a night when Lina hadn't been able to contact anyone for aid had been sheer terror and a suffocating feeling of helplessness. She shuddered even to think of it as an abstraction. Now imagine an entire planet of women who couldn't call in to authorities, and if they could, would have those authorities ignore them. Discount them. Maybe even make the situation worse.

No. That happened all too often on Earth. Somehow they'd correct the situation on Aldierra. They also had to see that all men who called into the emergency line were also treated fairly and got a quick response. This would be primarily on her shoulders.

She imagined a call center entirely composed of women. Maybe not take it that far, but half female, that would be good. But… how the heck would that call center work?

Twenty billion people.

They strolled the always-darkened halls of Legion HQ on Sarastor. Both Erik and she had to follow the colored lights on the glassy black wall that showed them the way to Legion Communications. The main offices were on the fifth floor of the mountain-sized building, though not near the residential quarters that were also on that level.

"I suppose this could be educational," Erik said. "I've never had the interest to look behind the scenes before. In front has been hectic enough. This is the kind of information that might come in handy sometime, though. Maybe."

Here was not where the communications between Legionnaires and their staff were handled. Those took place on much higher security levels. Rather, here emergency calls from across the sector were received and filtered for importance and targeting. Lina shook hands with the director, Ms. Wellering. Garbed in the pleated, tent-like fashion that Sarastorans favored, she nodded respectfully at Erik and gave Lina a curious look even as Lina glanced around. Machinery in the form of blinking consoles and solid light formed the walls of a smallish room, no larger than a normal dining room.

This served an entire galactic sector? Lina still wasn't sure just how much area that entailed, but a sector was huger than huge, with hundreds of inhabited solar systems. Space was *big*. Planets held a lot of people, and planets weren't the only places that had large populations Out Here. She'd read as well of space stations the size of small planets.

Surely Lina could get a feel for how Aldierran distress calls should be handled. They had nine months before they had to expand to three worlds' worth.

Lon and Jae had arranged for communications satellites and for the military to handle calls, but Lina had convinced them that this was another aspect they'd have to take over, at least partially.

Wellering monitored the feed by looking at the sparkles within various rainbows that held limited spectra. She controlled it by wiggling her fingers as if she had a hidden keyboard, shrugging her shoulders, and rolling her eyes this way and that. It was the technique of Sarastoran communication with computers, something Lina was only beginning to learn.

Wellering told them that as the mega-policing force for the sector, the Legion received millions of calls for help every day. The vast majority were rerouted to local authorities. Legion outposts were set deep in space. Small Legion offices were located on each major member planet of the AffSys where they could receive quick response. When an uncontrollable threat was reported, the main Legion ranks were called upon to respond. Headquarters here on Sarastor contained vast hangars of crazy-fast hyperdrive ships as well as a wealth of weaponry that could be added to the Legionnaires' powers to subdue an enemy or counter natural disasters.

"How long did it take to put all this together?" Lina waved her arms to take in the room's magical-seeming machinery. "Do you think we could cobble something like it in a few days or a month, to serve a population of twenty billion?" She added, "Our emergencies will mostly be social ones. Environmental ones."

"Riots and wars," Erik put in. He nudged her. "Even I know that much, and I've only glanced at Neutrino's reports."

Lina sighed. "I don't want to think about those. But that doesn't mean they don't exist. Yes, riots and wars and domestic abuse and ethnic cleansing and plagues, for all I know."

The director shook her head as she puzzled the problem. Her fingers moved, and some sparkles across the room responded. "This has been built upon for over two hundred years, Mrs. Valiant."

Lina tried not to wince at the title. Legion regs were specific about what people were called in public, to make sure their ranks were respected. She tried to remember everyone's costume names in front of this stranger.

Wellering continued, "It's always been state of the art. You don't achieve this overnight."

No, you didn't. But they needed something *now*. This had to be done, and done right. "Is there any emergency system in the AffSys that uses people to answer calls in some way? I don't mean an all-human system, but people with computers backing them up?"

"Very old fashioned." Wellering's chin drew back into her neck, as if she wanted to avoid telling her visitors that this was a terrible idea.

"Old fashioned," Erik murmured to himself. "Any of your predecessors still around? Someone we could talk to? Maybe someone from a hundred years ago?"

"A hundred years?" Lina blinked at Erik. Right, people lived long lives Out Here. How long were they? She grabbed Erik's arm. "Are there people like that? Someday I'll get used to all this. That's a great idea, Er– I mean, Sunstorm. Where do we find them?"

Lina thought she'd read that Wiley was pretty old, though he looked comfortably middle-aged. Old people might be the trick here at that, though the Worlds needed to get the latest tech asap. Starting out they'd take what they could. Speaking of Wiley…

"Does Dr. Mem-Bazer–" it was crazy here in Legion HQ not to call him "Wiley" – "have any sub-sub laboratories? Non-official ones? I got the impression that he had some staffs that weren't associated with the Legion at all. Maybe he has computer people he could lend us?"

She touched her right earring. "Wiley? Are you listening anywhere? I just need one of your minds. Oh good. Could you review what we've been talking about, offer some advice or some people? Thank you. I need this info tomorrow morning, local time, from wherever it is we're staying. Yes, thanks again."

She turned to Erik and Wellering. "Now, about those predecessors. I love that idea. Who can we talk to right now?"

# 10

Her visit had been productive, but Lina had hit the sack hard after their return. It seemed a long while later that she woke, likely from a gentle, timed stim. She could think again. She felt clear. She felt rested. She rolled over as easily as she could, but the arm around her shifted, and he touched her lightly, stroking the line of her shoulder. Such a safe feeling.

"Morning, angel," Jae said softly. "Did you sleep well? No bad dreams?"

"What a wonderful thing sleep is," she said, turning so she could look into those amazing blue eyes of his. "Good morning, darling stranger… I mean, Jae." She met his lips with her own.

Oh yes, wonderful Jae liked to sleep in the nude. She ran her hands over his warm skin, feeling the hard curves of him, how he breathed, how his heart beat. Such amazing creatures, men. Such a wonderful, wonderful man Jae was.

His golden hair fell around his shoulders, bristly but soft, like thick fur on a ginger cat. Not at all like Londo's silken hair, so much shorter than Jae's. Her fingers paused in their exploration. Londo wasn't here. She could sense him flying somewhere on this world, talking to someone and quite oblivious to her.

"Lon volunteered for my second shift," Jae said as he leaned in to nibble under her ear. He eased the nightgown's strap from her shoulder and followed its trail.

Lina swallowed and tried not to choke as she caught her breath. This was just Jae and her. He was her husband now.

"Um, um… Wait a minute. Ah–"

Jae eased back to regard her. One of his masked expressions almost slid into place. But not quite. "No, Lon's not here. I happened to mention that you and I were missing something, and he agreed with me." His eyes sparkled and he gave her a lopsided, hopeful little smile, waiting for her invitation. "Are we good?"

Jaeson Rallene was the most beautiful man in Creation. He was lying beside her now. Naked. Her legal husband. They had never consummated their marriage, not as a twosome.

Jae's lovely wide mouth beckoned. His soft jawline was unmarred by a single whisker that could scratch her. And under the sheet lurked a body fashioned like a god. He was absolutely, completely perfect.

Lina gulped. "I sh-should take a shower first." Lina turned to roll out of bed.

But he grabbed her wrist and pulled her back. "We'll be all hot and sweaty in a few minutes," he told her. "We can both take a shower afterward."

He gathered her to himself, pulling her nightgown with her inside. His lips descended onto her mouth. She breathed his fresh breath as he tasted her.

Ohmigosh, she probably had morning breath.

Lina pushed away. "I need to brush my teeth. I need to comb my hair. I need to lose ten pounds." *I need to make myself perfect for you.* What had she done, to marry a perfect man? What had she been thinking? Lina Muttbutt had no business–

"Shut up," Jae whispered in her ear. He pulled her arms above her head so she couldn't move and trapped her in another perfect kiss.

The world started to spin and from here, its center, Lina could hear Jae speaking without words... to what? The universe? No – her mouth. Where Jae's tongue swept through her mouth, exploring, he left a trail of freshness.

It was like going to the dentist for a cleaning, only there was no grit and it was a helluva lot more arousing. Lina laughed, her giggles swallowed up by Jae. When he released her, she covered her lips with two fingers but had to laugh again.

"Londo has a breath spray he uses sometimes," Jae told her. He leaned down and huffed into her nose.

His breath now reeked of peppermint.

Lina burst out laughing and Jae joined her. "I'm sorry," she finally said. "I've messed this up, haven't I?"

"I'm not perfect, Lie-Lie. Don't think of me that way."

"But you're so beautiful."

"And so are you."

She blushed in wonder. He really believed that of her.

Jae ran his thumb over her chin, examining her face, her lips, before gazing into her eyes. "You're my little barbarian bride. I choose you, now and forever. However you are."

"And you're civilized."

"Oh yes, they've civilized me." He eased down to join her on her pillow and gently caught a fistful of her curling auburn hair. "Remind me how it was to be barbarian, Terran. We were wed in the old ways. Barbarian ways to the rest of the sector."

"I thought Feith was so advanced?"

He held a length of her hair up so she could see it, too. The lock bounced and steadied into a long curlicue. "We live on a spiral path. Feith was a level above that of Earth, but both apparently facing in the same direction, dealing with similar issues. We are attuned, you and I." He let the curl fall across Lina's bare shoulder. His hand followed it down to the dropped strap, then down farther, pulling her bodice off one breast and then spreading his fingers to cup her.

"Time to learn how to harmonize with each other, wife."

How his gaze could penetrate her soul! She shivered under the heat, in awe of the power he radiated, drawing her to him. She ran her palm over the side of his face, so different from Londo's, and then rose up to meet his mouth with her own.

Such sweetness. Such coiled energy, primed for sudden release. This was Jae.

Lina pressed herself tighter to him. She sought his mind and after a moment's hesitation, it opened slightly to her. She'd take whatever he offered her. But–

There were other minds...

It was she who broke the kiss. "I really, really hate to say this, love," she said, "but we're surrounded by telepaths. I'm not sure how well we're shielding."

Jae paused and his eyes unfocused. They came back and he smiled at Lina. "It seems even Tishana don't shield too well under those circumstances," he said, paying attention to her collarbone with his fingers. "What's her name– Sweeney? and your friend David... Here, are you still wearing that Ruby?" His hand fumbled between her breasts, detaching the tape that held it in place.

He rolled over, depositing the palm-sized stone on the nightstand. "I think it'll be safe enough for a little while over here." He gave it a pat. "You just sleep and don't mind anything we do. That should go for everyone else as well." And he turned back to embrace his bride.

"But honey, the kids'll hear," Lina warned even as he rolled her onto her back.

"Let the children take care of themselves. Didn't Mart and Gorgeon recommend exercise to increase the efficacy of the stims?" Jae nuzzled his way down her neck.

"Um. Hard exercise, do you think?"

"We can always experiment. Now hush, woman, so I can concentrate."

Later Jae and she clung together, swaying skin to skin to a slow dance song. He was surprisingly shy, his mind burrowing curiously into hers and then holding back from her own intrusion. Despite his showman exterior, he was an extremely private person. He apologized twice for proceeding too roughly, and apologized again for not being open himself.

"Something I'll have to work on," he told her with a guilty half-smile.

Ordinarily Lina might insist on him working on it right now, but there were too many minds waking up and Jae wasn't nearly adept yet at guarding his thoughts from others. Plus Lina wasn't really a master of that either. She settled for nestling her head under his chin and closed her eyes in contentment. At least now she understood him more than she had. She resonated to him as a wife should. He was far more than friend, but they weren't yet completely certain how to act around each other.

He was so vulnerable, so strong. So tender. Londo had surprised her with the depth of emotion that he could feel and here was Jae, just as deep, just as eager to love. Lina had always thought that men weren't capable of loving like a woman did. How wrong she had been!

Jae was delicious and loved to be teased, so she did and he laughed and laughed with her. She could feel the tensions in him, the worries, the fears, drain out of him as they held each other so closely. Her trusty old boom box reached the end of the CD and silence hung in the room. Still they swayed to music unplayed.

"I love you," they both said together, and that made them laugh some more.

With Londo she felt so elemental, as if she could reach out and shake the universe. He was the deep of the ocean, the center of a thunderstorm. And with Jae she felt – released. Free to fly, free to touch the stars. Jae was starlight on that ocean. He was the sun coming out after the storm. With him she felt as if the heavens were just out of reach but smiling down upon her.

She smoothed back Jae's hair. "You shouldn't hide these," she said as she traced his narrow, pointed ears. "They're so elegant." His hair fell back and she brushed it, first to push it away from his ears, and then just to feel its thick fullness, so much like a cat's.

He hummed the tune they had been swaying to. "Sweet angel," he murmured.

"Jae honey."

"Must I be?" His steps paused and she looked up at him.

"You're both 'honey.' The cats are all 'honeys.'"

"I want something. Unique."

He'd told her earlier that evening that she was his 'angel' due to her middle name, Angelina.

"These things come with time," she said.

He cocked his head at her. "You've got a name for Londo..."

"'Teddy,'" she said. "For Teddy Roosevelt, a President who went around saying, 'Bully! Bully!' which means… uh, I think 'this is great stuff!' It's not used that way anymore. But it can also mean…"

"A person who bullies." Jae ran his tongue around a cheek as he thought. "This is good?"

"It's also for Ours."

A look of partial comprehension came over Jae's face. Ours had been the beloved toy that had kept Londo sane through much of his childhood imprisonment. "How does that connect?"

"Ours was a teddy bear, a soft, stuffed toy for children. Teddy bears were named after Teddy Roosevelt." She smiled into his chest. "We'll have to watch the Paddington Bear movies together. You'll love teddy bears. They're cuddly and cute."

"A two-sided name." He considered and nodded. "Very good. It fits him."

"Jaeson." She rubbed his shoulder and strong arm. "That's a Biblical name if you spell it right. Or mythological: Jason and the Argonauts."

"Argonauts?"

"I'll get a book and find the story for you. Did he have anything to do with the kraken? 'Release the kraken!' is a good thing to yell when things get boring. Let's see. Jaeson." She brushed his hair again; it was luscious. "Jaeson the Tom Cat. A tom is a male cat." She laughed. "You've spent your life working off all that sexual steam and parading your glory around the neighborhood, just like a tom."

"Parading...?"

"You strut on occasion. You perform to the public as a goofy way of hiding your true self. That's amazing. You're a natural showman, just like Lon, but... but..." She tried to compare and contrast. "He plays to the crowd. You play to the world."

Jae laughed.

"You do. You're a tom cat."

She shrieked as he maneuvered her into a deep dip that caught her unawares. A squirm dropped her the short distance to the floor and Jae pounced upon her, quieting her with hot kisses and long caresses.

"Ooo. Come and lay at my hearth, Tom Cat," she cooed.

"My wife," Jae breathed in her ear. "Suddenly it feels like that, like we're really married. It's different."

"We needed this. Three is fun. Three is–" She didn't know how to put it. "But two is deeper. Two is so much more intimate."

"I can go farther with you this way," Jae said. "When we merge minds, we contrast and compare. We can experiment with our selves. Safely."

"Is that what we're doing? And when we're three, we balance out and yet…"

"Exactly. But we also…"

Lina clapped one hand against the other, then let the arm arc out. "We expand. We break the boundaries together."

They lay there, considering.

"Do you think it'll be like this fifty years from now?"

He touched her lips with a finger. "No," he said. "It will be even better. I can't imagine that, better than this. But it will."

"I love you, Jaeson. I will always love you, beyond forever."

"Beyond eternity. Into the heart of creation, angel. Together we'll make new worlds."

"New hope."

"New dreams."


"Lina! For shame!" David was waiting for her in the teaching hall before class that morning. He drew her aside. "I can't believe you!"

"David!" she admonished back. "With an alien!"

"You, too! An alien who's not your husband!" "I can't believe you – of all people – would do–"

"Take a look over there, David. And keep secrets."

David looked confused, and then followed the line of sight from Lina's nudge out into the auditorium filling with attendees. Neutrino and Valiant were both utilizing their privilege as Three Worlds sponsors to scarf up some tasty calories at the snack table before they ported to Aldierra.

Neutrino looked up, directly at David. And gave David the finger with a devilish grin on his face. Valiant said something to him, shaking his head, and Neutrino clearly said "Oh," though David couldn't hear him from this distance. Then Neutrino changed the extended finger to the ring finger of his right hand.

Subtly, Valiant pointed to something on that finger. A ring. And Valiant raised the ring finger of his left hand.

And then both went back to gobbling snacks as if nothing had happened. It had been so quick, it took several moments for the message to sink in.

"Holy eff," David whispered. He blinked once, twice. "Holy, holy– You can't–"

"It's absolutely legal and it's on a need-to-know basis only. For now," Lina told him softly. "We don't think some people would understand."

"Holy eff they wouldn't," David breathed. "Did I ever tell you you were a crazy Sagittarian, Lina?"

"Only about a million times."

# 11

Londo and Jae had cleared their Legion schedules in time to allow them the Aldierran port before the morning class began. They didn't want to interrupt a class session to have Lina port them back so instead they had time to scout the world on a wider basis than Jae had previously been able to do.

The entire planet was a disaster that unveiled itself in bleak detail as they flew a thousand feet over it.

"I want to check out that big black spot," Lon said of an area on a global map he'd noticed. "I didn't like it. It was unnatural."

"We'll go there tomorrow maybe. It's in another hemisphere. Where are we?"

They attempted to coordinate their maps with satellite signals.

"We need better GPS, communications on all levels. Planetary transporters."

"We'll get that all eventually."

"Within the week."

Jae grimaced. Time constraints. "Let's try for full communications tomorrow, maybe leave the transporters for the day after we officially begin. That way we can get them done right."

Londo nodded and then caught his breath. He pointed past the horizon. A river. The continent-sprawling city – now consisting of low buildings with occasional patches of agricultural area – went right up to the water's edge. And far, far upriver, visible only by Londo's paravision:

A dam had broken.

"It must have just happened. I'll get–"

"I'll handle preliminary rescues," Jae told him as he saw the situation through Londo's mind. "Do what you can water-wise."

With that they both took off at top speed across the sky.

Lon's natural flight was faster than a Legion Array could provide, so he sped ahead of Jae. The ground zoomed up at him as he dove and grabbed a chunk of a sturdy enclosing structure that only held machinery. He used it as a dike to funnel the waters into the riverbed.

Again and again he ripped long lengths of materials, smashing them into the ground so they wouldn't be torn apart from the force of the water. Entire vacant buildings came down under his touch, rebuilt into a high-banked channel that wouldn't solve the problem but might work well enough until he could attack the true one.

Jae swooped and swooped again, grabbing people caught in the rushing flood and dragging them well past Lon's work. "Run!" he shouted at them when he set them down, as that channel could not hold for long.

As soon as he saw someone flailing, there would be others as well. One time he emerged from the water with five people hanging off him. His Array could handle it all, but his bones and muscles strained.

He missed catching some people. But he rescued many others. People on shore were trying to help as well, holding out sticks and throwing ropes and floating devices for the drowning to latch onto. The roar of the churning water covered the screams.

Lon turned from his makeshift repair and headed to the dam. Three large blocks of it had dissolved completely; it was earthen. Earthen! A dam of this size!

He blew coldness hard onto its one side and relaxed an iota when a thick sheet of ice formed under the top water. Then he repeated the action twice more. That cut much of the flood.

Vehicles that had bulldozing as at least part of their purpose sat in a lot nearby. He picked up one's curved blade and dragged it across a stretch of farmland. Over and over, he carried loads of dirt to the dam, freezing it into large masses as he placed it so not much was lost in the currents. He wrenched thick girders of metal from more buildings and used them to stomp upon over the dirt, compacting and then supporting it even more.

Then he flew off but returned almost immediately with truckloads of boulders. They went in upstream of the dam, in whole as well as shattered form, and he compressed more dirt around them to create a sturdy barrier. The resulting dam was a good fifteen feet higher than the original must have been, and it was holding in the flood. In his opinion, it would do so until real repairs could be made.

Now he had time to aid Jae. It took but a second to find him.

On a bank behind one of his barriers a pile of drowned bodies lay around Jae. He stood above them, his eyes closed and arms outstretched. Giving a nod to himself that Jae was handling things, Londo took off to find more victims, though mostly he found the dead.

When he finally returned, Jae was crouched next to two women who looked as if they were still half-swooning from their ordeal. More like near death. Londo had seen Jae do this before: change the water in people's lungs into oxygen. Change carbon dioxide in their blood into oxygen as well. It worked for many, but not all. It apparently had worked for all but a few here. He thought that Jae was instructing something to warm the women as well. Was he commanding their bodies as a whole to do so, or was he warming the tissue that made up their bodies?

As noisy emergency vehicles finally screamed into the area and flying vehicles of various sizes hovered overhead, Lon drew near. Jae spoke to the women. One of them was so old Londo would have called her a crone if it hadn't been impolite. The other was middle-aged, or perhaps much younger but worn from her ordeal. Or life. Her nose had been chopped off, but the damage had been made long ago. Both had hollow cheeks, bad teeth with gaps. Their skin showed signs of malnourishment and disease. And they constantly coughed.

Londo didn't think it all came from swallowing too much water.

They shrank from Londo as he descended from the sky, hiding their faces from him. Their clothing was rags, made worse from the flood. And wonder of wonders, they also seemed to ease away from Jae, though he held one of the crone's hands and spoke softly to her.

"Where is your family?" he asked her. "We need to find someone to care for you until you're well. Don't you have family?"

The crone burst out crying. She wore Jae's cape, but snatched her hand away from his.

Londo crouched down as well. "Why are you trying to hide?" he asked the younger woman. She didn't let her hands drop from where they hid her eyes. "Don't be afraid of us."

She lowered her head and used her hands to cup the crown of her head, the bit of her that faced Londo.

"We want to help you." He made his voice as gentle as he could. He took off his vest to offer it to her.

"I think their family was caught in the flood," Jae told him as the translator gave his words to the women. Its vocabulary was still at such a preliminary, learning stage. "Something about other women."

"Women's quarters–" the noseless one managed to say.

"A special building?" Jae asked her.

She gave a quick nod.

"Um. Women live separate from the men?"

"F-family compound."

"Where are the men?"

Both women shrugged as if it were unimportant.

"But the women–"

Lon said, "They were in a building? Couldn't they get out? Or did the water come in too fast for them to escape?"

"Locked in. Locked in." The woman began to rock back and forth. "All gone. My little granddaughter– She was about to give birth. Any day now. She was so scared, and now this."

The crone set up a wail even as Londo leaped into the sky.

After only a few minutes Lon returned. He shook his head at Jae.

"I'm… sorry," Jae finally told the women. "Is there a safe place we can leave you? For tonight? We could take you to hospital."

That caused the noseless one to glance at him, anger in her eyes. "What hospital takes women?" she demanded to know. "What safe place is there for women?"

Londo looked around. He hadn't noticed it, but there'd only been a handful of women among the hundreds rescued. Where were this world's women?

"I know a safe place," he told them. "With doctors who will see to you. Soft beds. Good food. Clean air."

Jae reached out to take the elder's hand again. "It will be peaceful."

She stopped her wails at that and looked at him as if she couldn't understand the concept.

"Lina," Londo said to the air. "An emergency; sorry to interrupt. We'll have two extra coming back with us. Can you port us directly? Get someone there to give you a picture for a target. Get Mart. Have him find an extra suite and meals for two adults for at least two nights."

"More likely a week," Jae said as the women gaped at the men who talked to air.

"Give us a half-hour before then," Londo instructed his wife, many parsecs away. "I need to bring in more emergency vehicles and transport some of the victims to medical treatment."

Hundreds lived that day who would have otherwise died, thanks to Lon and Jae and the people of the river who rushed to help.

"Lina does not come here alone," Londo announced to Jae as the four, now five as they had been joined by another female survivor, also lost, prepared to port back to Traim. He finished making a memo about the trip for his wife to go through when she had time that night. He ended it with, "They don't trust men. You'll have to be the one who leads the effort to find out what's going on with the female population here."

Jae chewed on his lips a moment, thinking. "Not alone? She was chosen for this as much as we were. But yes, we need to choose a guard unit for her."

"One that has access to fast transport. Make that three or more teams. She can't use all her energy trying to port a group of people with her. They'll have to scramble to keep up. We'll station them at equidistant points across the globe."

"We'll have our own transporter system in place soon." Jae checked his own notes, adding them to Lon's for both his spouses to read. "I'll check with Wiley. He can get his assistants to speed things up on that front. Along with programming our communication and surveillance satellites."

"We need those last ready by tomorrow morning. This project has to get going, stat."

"Agreed. We'll have Lina port you here tomorrow when she wakes up. By the time she's finished her morning routine…?"

Londo nodded. "I'm not sure how long that takes, but whatever it is, I'll put them in place. Just make sure she's awake enough to port me back. I don't want to be stranded on this world too long." He shuddered. "We really have to fix all this?"

Jae's own world had been destroyed when he could do nothing about it. That would never happen again. "This world will not die under our watch," he declared with all the power of his being.

He turned to the other passengers and suggested they hold hands, warning once again that there would be pitch black for at least two minutes. Instead of doing that, they huddled together. Jae reached out to lay his hand upon the crone's shoulder. She shook when he did that, but did not argue. Then the blackness overcame them.


The light hit all at once, blinding, and the women screamed, clutching each other tighter.

"Sorry," Lina's voice called out.

They'd expanded the Traim hotel's medical room for the occasion with a short line of cubicles containing beds. It didn't hold all the specialty equipment a true hospital would contain, but it had enough.

Lina was in her full white Tour costume with pretty green ribbons, its loose material floating with her every movement. Along with an assistant and Subcommander Andri, Doctor Mart assessed the arrivals behind Lina, who held out three marbles. "Translators for everyone," she said brightly as she launched them to hover next to each woman.

Lon and Jae were filthy, well-coated with dried mud and ick. Lina supposed it was part of their job. Unfortunately, the women were as well. An assistant passed out wipes to the women first, while Londo and Jae helped themselves to her supply.

"How are you feeling?" Lina asked the women. She helped the oldest wipe her face. "Let's have you all sit. Here are some drinks. They have a bit of tranquillizers in them, but nothing major. You've been through hell, I hear. I'm so sorry. So very sorry."

After they'd stared open-mouthed at their new location, the eyes of the women settled upon Lina. They fell to their knees. They lowered their heads to the ground, gibbering.

"Oh jeez," Lina said and glanced at her husbands.

Andri stepped in to raise the elder woman. "Hello," she told her kindly, hearing that the marble was translating fairly well. "I'm Nurunori, the subcommander of the Affiliated Systems Mega Legion. We are glad you're still among the living. It was a very close call, from what I heard."

She nestled the lady into a chair with a blanket around her, and the female assistant whom Lina thought was a non-hero aide to Andri handed her a drink. Londo and Jae did the same for the others as Lina ducked about, trying to catch the women's gazes when they refused to look at her.

She knew that Aldierran skin came in different shades of an orange that was brighter than Earth's peachy-browns, but the skin of all three seemed subdued, tinged with gray.

"I'm the Speaker for Aldierra," she told them. "I guess you knew that. You must have seen me when I was channeling the world to everyone. It was probably pretty scary for you. That was Aldierra herself doing that; I was just along providing the transportation. Which means you don't have to bow to me or anything. I'm a regular person. She's the one who knows everything about you. Well, I did too as it was going on, but by now I've forgotten."

The women tried to hide within the blankets Jae and Lon had handed out, even as they groaned from their injuries and loss. "Breathe," Lina told them, trying not to sound authoritarian. "You've been through so much today. Take some deep breaths. That's good. And another one. Please.

"You can call me Lina. Have Jae and Londo introduced themselves? They're the Minister and Protector of Aldierra, you should know. Did you see the announcement? Did you recognize them? They're famous, but Aldierra is far away from most of the places they're famous in. This man here is Doctor Mart. He knows everything about medicine and he's going to get you as well as he can while you're here. He's not going to hurt you in any way, and–" she raised her eyebrows to the doctor meaningfully– "he'll explain what he's doing as he does it. If not before. Now, what are your names?"

That proved a tough question. The women had man-names, names the men in their – family? village? It seemed larger than just a family – called them.

Jae set his arms across his chest and frowned at the noseless one. "I'm not calling you that. That's demeaning."

"It's because of my nose," the woman said as she cupped her hand over it to hide it.

"I don't care. Why hasn't that been seen to? Fixed?"

"My mother did it."

"Your mother–!"

"She did it to save me. She told me I was a pretty child."

The third woman in the group ventured to speak. "You do not want to be pretty. It attracts attention."

The non-Aldierrans all looked at each other.

"Your mothers must have given you names," Andri surmised. "If your true names are secret," she then ventured, "we can gift you with new ones. Will that be all right?"

Lina beamed at her. How perceptive! Secret names – that was exactly what was going on.

So the women became Dawn – the noseless one – and Spring and Hope, the crone. They had the meanings of their new names explained to them. They liked them.

Dr. Mart tried to be as unobtrusive as possible while he eased from woman to woman, setting sensors upon each as they flinched from his touch. His features became unreadable as he took in the readings.

**That can't be good,** Londo commented silently, and Jae nodded agreement at him. The doctor clearly didn't want the patients to see he was overly concerned.

They got the women to eat some nutritious gruel as Andri's assistant flitted about, acting like an attentive server. Lina determined that she should learn her name, since it wasn't offered. The assistant seemed quite attached to Andri, following her facial hints as to what needed to be done.

"How were you caught in the flood?" Andri asked them. Lon and Jae stayed back, out of the women's line of sight. "Did you have any warning?"

"My daughters!"

"My sisters!"

"My mother!"

And cousins and friends, all female. Spring's hysteria erupted with a vengeance. Dawn and Hope followed her, crying for their own reasons. Their bodies shook hard. They couldn't stop or breathe well between the sobs, and hard coughs didn't help the situation.

"May I?" Lina held out her arms and Spring didn't say no. So Lina hugged her, the closest one to her. Andri hugged Hope. At a nod from Andri, the assistant hugged the third.

"There we go. There we go," Andri crooned to them.

"D-daughters." Spring tried to say more, but couldn't.

Mart administered tranquilizer shots as discreetly as he could, but it was a full ten minutes before the episodes began to abate.

Lina glanced at her husbands. Londo shook his head. **I couldn't find any more survivors along the river,** he told her silently. **There were entire compounds of just women and girls under water, mud, and destroyed walls. All dead. Now I know why.**

Jeez, he saw this kind of thing every day. Lina wondered how paraheroes, especially the mega ones like her husbands, could take it. They had on-call therapists to help, at least.

"I'm so sorry," Lina told the women again. "I'm afraid your families are gone."

Though at times they could barely speak, the women managed to tell a cohesive, if limited story. Their female relatives had been locked into structures where they couldn't escape the waters. The imprisonment was a normal experience. Everyday life. These three had just happened to be outside at the time, able to run with the men as the river surged down upon them.

Women were kept locked up because if they weren't, they'd run away, not knowing to where. "Anywhere would be better," Hope assured Andri. "Even if we died on our journey. Death would be better."

"These ladies need to rest," Mart ordered. He looked not to Andri but to Lina for direction. This was Three Worlds business.

"Right," Lina said. The tranquillizers were obviously kicking in now. The women were looking around instead of clinging to them. "And to top things off on this terrible day, you're in a strange place. This technology is probably foreign to you. Are you feeling a little better now? I hate to have you stand…"

Londo murmured in her ear and she relayed the message. "Oh. These chairs can move. I'm new to all this too, you should know. It's pretty crazy when you first arrive in all this technology, but it's neat and I hope you enjoy it once you settle in. Let's get a quick tour."

The chairs followed her as Mart and she showed the women the cubicles available for them, and that each had a bathroom.

"Just ask 'computer' if you have any questions," Lina told them. "The very first question I asked was, 'How the heck do you use this bathroom?'" She tried to laugh and the women seemed to relax in mutual understanding, or perhaps it was the tranquilizers kicking in further. "Computer showed me how. It was pretty graphic but it got the job done. Now I love these kinds of bathrooms. There are some surprises but you'll wind up liking them."

The aide handed fluffy robes to Jae and he handed them out. "If you have enough energy now to shower–"

The women looked at him blankly.

Ah. Lina said, "A shower is like a standing bath. The water comes down from above you, and it drains out in the floor. You don't have to sit in dirty water. Oh, and you can control the water temperature. I'm sure the soap here smells lovely too. You can ask 'computer' to do the soaping for you if you want."

Jae nodded. "Shower. Right. Well, as you shower your robes will be cleaned for you, so you don't have to put on dirty clothing afterward."

"You can choose new clothing in the morning," Andri assured them. "I'm sure you'll find something you like."

"We will have counselors then as well," Mart put in. "Female ones. And female doctors."

"I hear therapy is very good Out Here," Lina confided to the women, although she could feel both her husbands mentally poking her that she needed to take her own advice.

Jae put his hand on Lina's shoulder. "Add twenty minutes to tonight's dinner," he said quietly. "We need to have a meeting. By then our people will have checked in from Aldierra. We need to add all this to what we've learned."

"We have people?" Lina asked.

"And we'll have a lot more before this is over."

"A *lot*," Londo added for emphasis.

The door chimed and Lina checked her watch. "That's for me," she explained to the women. "I'm so, so sorry. I've got to go. But Lon and Jae will give me a full rundown of everything. I leave you in their hands – you can trust them, even if they're men – as well as the subcommander's." She spared a quick glance down at her now-filthy outfit and shrugged to herself. "I'll need to change first.

"In the next few days I want us all to sit down and have a long talk about your world and what's going on there. We will arrange decent burials for your loved ones and see that you have safe homes to relocate to.

"But we need to understand what's happening on Aldierra. I had guessed we'd need women's shelters but it looks like that will get run up to one of our first priorities. We are going to change things for the better for every living thing on your world, very much including its women." She shook her index finger at them for emphasis. "You can bet money on that."

As the door closed behind her, Andri said, "She's changing the paths of hundreds of worlds right now." As an afterthought she said, "I've been thinking that the Tour should stay here for one more day."

Londo and Jae looked at each other before nodding.

Andri dipped her chin at them. "I'll arrange the particulars."

Mart announced, "You ladies should see if you can rest. The nannites you've ingested can work best if you're asleep. Your food had tranquilizers; we told you that, didn't we? Yes. So sleep as you can. Heal."

"Here's a signal you can use when you're ready for visitors tomorrow," Andri told them. "Until then, no one will bother you unless you get up hungry and want food. Then use this." She showed them the system. The Legionnaires left the room.

"You're going to save this Aldierra, are you?" Andri asked Londo and Jae once the door closed behind them. "Good luck with that."

# 12

Anger coursed through Rikli-En's gut, but he reined it back hard so that it merely bubbled redly in the back of his mind. He had not been allowed to participate, to learn the process of undoing Mind Control. The planetary officials who made reservations for the seminar had recognized him, broken into his comm circuit, and respectfully informed him that he was ineligible.

"This is for those who will be using the actual process, or teaching others in turn to do it," they tried to explain to him, "not for casual observation. Sir."

*Sir.* They had called him *Sir*, as if he were an ordinary person and not Heir Apparent to the Imperial throne.

He objected vehemently. He told them he had a duty to his citizenry to learn. "Sir," they insisted, "if you wish, you may send someone who will be doing this work on your worlds, and we will squeeze them in. We're holding extra classes, but we cannot guarantee this will continue, as some of the sessions have been… sporadic. Even so, they are filling up fast, if they aren't full already. At this point…" they checked their schedules, "we have only five spots left; that's all unless there's another class after the nine-day mark. We are otherwise filled to capacity. All the classes, even with these extra days. We do not reasonably expect you ever to do this kind of work. Please understand."

He did not, but he also was intelligent enough to recognize a stone wall when he saw one. On occasion being important had its drawbacks.

He crooked his finger at one of his bodyguards and the man, Hammon, advanced to his camera's range, bowing his head in servility. "This is my chosen representative," Rikli-En told the officials. "He will be handling the process on my worlds. He will fill one seat."

The officials looked at him doubtfully, but they could not deny this person, not when Rikli-En had said this. For the vast Yanist-Glory Empire to send one person was not an unreasonable request.

As Jae approached, he could both feel and hear the flute through the sound-proofed auditorium. It was the end of session. The music seemed to bless him, clearing him out as if he'd just taken an invigorating shower. Others waiting to meet the participants stood a little straighter and began to smile at each other.

The doors opened. People began to pour out of the room, greeting with unveiled excitement the ones who had come. Jae waited for most of them to emerge before he went in. Lina looked up at him with that smile of hers as she dealt with some queries. Lon kept dutifully behind her when she exited the stage, checking the corners for any vestiges of trouble as he had undoubtedly done throughout the class he'd attended.

It was everywhere now, threat levels confusingly ranging from medium to severe. You were never sure just what you were walking into when you responded to a call. To make things worse, they'd been notified that Rikli-En was trying to worm his way into the classes. Would that mean the lecture hall would be safer or more dangerous than normal?

They had to make sure that Lina, the Terrans, and the Tishana were all kept away from it. They must be clear-minded to perform their best.

All Legionnaires were on top alert. Though dozens had been assigned Tour duty, they were now stretched too thin to see to it all. The idea of switching worlds was shelved completely; they'd remain here on Traim for the rest of the Tour and hunker down. More local security units had been added, but communications with them weren't up to Legion standards. Andri was supervising improving that. She'd whip the locals into shape.

There'd already been a handful of deaths. All terrorists, Jae was relieved to say. No Legionnaires had been seriously injured. So far.

Not just a dozen but a few handfuls of ships had been stopped at the spaceport because they either carried known terrorists or weaponry. A fight last night with one ship's crew had lit up the city's sky. From within their protected hotel, none of the Tour assistants would have seen it.

"Nap," Lina announced to the two of them as she reached out to touch Jae's arm in welcome. "I am off to bed now. Bed bed bed, bed-bed. One and one-half hours."

"No," Lon said. "You're off to lunch now. When's the last time you ate?"

"Um," Lina started, and stopped.

"You said you'd eat at a break," Jae prompted.

"She didn't. I gave her food and she didn't eat," Lon tattled.

"I play the flute at breaks now," she said. "It's really helping. Hard to eat and play at the same time."

"I don't think you had much breakfast," Lon said.

"I'd rather sleep than eat, love. The last timed stim is wearing off. You know how I get when that happens. Out like a light. You two go out and have a nice lunch. Didn't you say something about multiple rings for this planet, Jae?"

"Moons," Jae corrected. He glanced to his side to spot Wiley approaching.

"Moons then. Bring me back something, especially if it actually tastes good. Wake me up a little early. I'll eat whatever it is if you let me sleep until then."

Wiley was pointing his tricorder at her. It buzzed angrily at something. He grunted. "Stimulants need a live body to work on," he said. "Londo, make sure she eats something. Five hundred calories. At the *very* least. Every meal. Eight hundred would be better."

"I'll get a milkshake," Lina said.

"Fruit, vegetables, complex carbs, protein," Wiley ordered. "At least I don't have to tell you no alcohol. Lina, you tell your people to think extra healthy. The more they take care of themselves, the better the stims will work and we won't have them dropping all over the place before they're done."

"She'll get a short stim and then we're all going to eat," Londo declared.

Lina didn't argue with Team Leader. Instead, she turned to gather her assistants for a quick meeting before they left.

A remarkably realistic summer breeze blew through the balcony of the restaurant overlooking the city. Through video "skylights" showing the real scene above, a string of artificial moons moved across the sky from east to west, sparkling like diamonds against a background of silky rings.

The Legionnaires around the table found the food crispy and delicious. Mimik clicked happily as she ate and added to the informal conversation. Human food was usually so soft. They ignored Lina, asleep in her pod of a chair, and the Terran was oblivious to the sounds around her. Mimik felt secure enough to chat informally with her fellow Legionnaires.

"The short stim didn't work long. I think I need to put her to bed," Lon told them. "Anyone see any stasi-keeps? There's no reason for her meal to go to waste." He got up to investigate the restaurant's kitchen. A stasi-keeper would keep Lina's dinner as fresh as if it were just served.

"You think she got five hundred calories?" Neutrino called to him. His features showed an ease with Londo, something Mimik would expect from the long-time friend.

"Probably not."

The Feithi Legionnaire dug into the food on his plate. "She'll like the daibit," he told them. "She's been complaining about the blandness of texture and taste of the things she's tried. This is–" He held his eating tongs up to turn a bite's worth of food back and forth for examination. "It's creamy with a bit of crunch around the sides. And it tastes like whatever cooked it knew what they were doing. A shame she hasn't had a chance for anything really good before this."

"We had tuddlies the other week," Dr. Mem-Bazer reminded him.

Neutrino nodded. "I think she liked those. Lina," he urged as he held his tongs near her mouth. "Let's get some nutrition into you."

"Uv."

"Open your mouth and chew. You can chew for a minute or two, right?"

Her eyelids cracked open. She saw what he was trying to do and opened her mouth. She chewed what he put in.

"There," he cooed to her. Mimik had seen this expression used when Neutrino was trying to con someone into doing something they weren't supposed to do. Or was there more involved? "Now concentrate. How does it taste? Wake up so you can eat. How does it smell?"

"Uh, nice, I guess. Good."

"That's a good girl. Let's get another bite into you, shall we?"

He kept urging her and she kept trying. He directed specific questions to her about what she was eating, and gradually she blinked more awake.

Neutrino was a most effective negotiator.

Mimik watched as other conversation went on around her, her mandibles shifting slowly side by side as she compared the two humans interacting. She was the second in command of Londo's Alpha Team. When disguising herself as specific sentient beings, she had to observe their quirks and emotional expressions as well as culture in order to create the ultimate facsimile.

Lina smiled warmly if blearily at Neutrino, seeming to eat because she wanted to please him. They kept their gazes on each other, never looking away. Neutrino's head tilted toward Lina as he fed her. The eye areas of both of them seemed completely relaxed. Their nostrils were wide but not flared.

They were members of their own team. They were telepaths. How would human bonds show a difference if they were lovers?

Dr. Mem-Bazer glanced at them without registering interest. He had a reputation among those who knew him well that none of his five minds noticed minor-level personal interactions.

Neutrino used prescribed drugs to keep his manic side in line. Londo's wife was heavily on stims. That might also explain things. Might.

"Here we go." Londo hustled back with a newly plated dinner identical to the one Lina had been served, safely encased in a stasi-keep. "I got two servings. We can eat them together tomorrow."

Lina's smile turned to Londo with the same warmth as she'd displayed for Neutrino.

"You're eating Jae's dinner?" Lon checked Neutrino's plate and then his face before he nodded approval. "Good. Hope you don't mind me finishing up for you." With that, he set about eating Lina's food. He paused when she looked interested in what was there, and took up tongs to feed her like Neutrino had.

"It's good," she told him. "Thank you."

"Good," he repeated. "I told you it would be."

But soon she was drowsing off again.

"Lina. Lina."

Lina blinked at Londo's prod. Befuddledly she looked around. She must have seen that they were still in the restaurant. "Not even a bed," she groaned.

"I'm going to take you there now."

"Whatever," she said listlessly. "Do you think if I just pulled my hair back and didn't dry it before class, that I could get another five minutes of sleep?"

Dr. Mem-Bazer pulled his tricorder out and frowned at it. "Humans weren't built to stay on stims this long," he said. "Lina, you've been operating on stimulants for almost as long as I've known you."

"Tell me about it," she mumbled. "Stims good."

"I'm going to recommend that you and your staff continue, but with longer rest breaks. I know the next round of participants don't want to wait an instant, but a few extra hours aren't going to kill anyone."

"That sounds nice," Lina gave a weak smile. "Eight hours of sleep. Mmm."

"Ten." The doctor looked from Londo to Neutrino. He was certainly treating them as a team.

Lon's mouth set in a line. "I'll inform them," he said. Lina was drifting back to sleep. "I'll tell Dr. Benton to neutralize any remnants of the stims in everyone's systems tonight, if she hasn't already."

"Pay," Lina said dreamily.

"What?"

She blinked, obviously trying to wake up. "David, Sue… and someone else… were asking about pay the other day. I f'got. David tried… figure up how much they'd be making, but he wasn't sure if… got it right. I don't think…" She shook her head, blinked, and laughed. "I don't think," she concluded with a sleepy snort.

Neutrino reached for Lina's padd. "Let's see. They'd want to know in Terran currency, right?"

"Mmm. Dollars. American." She closed her eyes.

He punched a few figures in, checked on the computer nets, and cross-referenced for each planet they'd hit and the worlds that had sent representatives. "Three point four five million dollars, American," he finally announced. "Each."

"Huh shih," Lina murmured, half-conscious.

"And you're taking home about ten times that."

"'At's nice," she said as she leaned against Londo and closed her eyes. "We can get… nice bedspread."

Lon checked Neutrino's figures. "You must be dead on your feet as well. Or this app is *folle.* The decimal's off. I don't think the basic conversion is right," he said, and handed the padd to Wiley, who was holding out his hand and expectantly wiggling his fingers for it.

The doctor frowned at the device. He waved his fingers at it, this time communicating directly with the computer, then waved them some more, tapped one of his rings against the device. Finally he passed the padd back. Neutrino made little gasping noises at the final figure. Lon himself couldn't speak to announce the number.

Mimik checked the screen over Neutrino's shoulder. The number flowed on and on across the screen. "That's after expenses and taxes?" she asked in wonder. "Maybe I should learn how to teach this, too. It seems much cleaner than running around in the sewers I was in last month. And six months ago, there was an explosion at a waste treatment plant…"

"I hate it when that happens," Londo sympathized as he eased Lina out of her chair.

Neutrino didn't make a move to join them. "If you think that's bad," he interrupted, "then you should have been on Feling 4 last summer. It's the hottest day of the year, and we're all wearing as little as we can get away with and still sweating like we're in a steam bath…"

# 13

The bedroom was completely dark and silent, but something had wakened Londo. Lina lay beside him under his protective arm, her soft, deep breaths unworried by anything.

Something hard struck Lon on his bare shoulder. "Ouch!" he said involuntarily even as he sprang out of the bed, keeping himself between Lina and wherever the projectile had come from.

"You're dead, Rand," a whispered voice laughed from the darkness. "Poison dart, instantaneous. Too bad."

Lon reached out a steel-hard arm and grabbed the intruder by his shirt, keeping him at arm's length and pulling him behind him as he opened the bedroom door. He tossed the assassin onto the carpet of the next room. The man rolled with the force of the throw, coming up smoothly to face him.

"Dammit, Kuttr–!" Londo began as soon as he'd closed the door behind him. *"Ostie!"*

"I see we'll have to schedule all kinds of new lessons for you," the man said with a triumphant grin. He looked at the trickle of blood that had oozed from Lon's small shoulder wound before it had closed up. When Londo touched Lina, his invulnerability clicked off. "If I didn't see it with my own eyes, I'd never have believed it."

He straightened and brushed himself off. "This now puts you in very real danger, Rand."

"Starhart."

"Whatever. What if you're with her in a crowd and someone decides that they really don't like what you're wearing that day? One shot and you're dead. Or can you turn it on and off as you like?" The Legion's combat chief settled onto the couch while Londo crossed his arms across his chest and scowled at him.

"No. That's one reason why we're never going to make any kind of public announcement as to how we... do what we do," Lon said angrily. "Kuttr, Lina needs her sleep. Even you with your thick head can see the importance of what she's doing here."

"Oh yes, important, very important," Kuttr said as he examined his nails. "Sleeping away while assassins lurk outside your door, just waiting for you to leave." Kuttr reached for some small pieces of mail that were piled on an end table. Only ceremonial messages were printed on paper. "Or they just send you invitations. 'Please, dear Starharts, honor us by appearing arm in arm at our latest soiree.' And then they don't bother to tell you that all the other guests will be bringing blasters."

"I'm sure it doesn't impress you at all, but we have discussed this," Londo fumed. He plopped down on the couch, bringing his legs up crossed in tailor fashion as he glared. "We'll try to keep an eye on touching in very crowded areas..."

"Oh, they're gonna *try*..." Kuttr rolled his eyes at the ceiling.

"And in any kind of dangerous situation, there's no touching at all. Lina will have her spirit guides pay attention to possible dangers..."

"And *guides*. How quaint." Kuttr sneered at him as he clinked his Legion ring against the end table. He always acted as if it were a nervous habit, but Londo had figured out years ago that the Legion's martial trainer did it merely to annoy.

"Londo?" The bedroom door opened and a very sleepy Lina appeared, clutching a robe to herself over a lace nightgown. It almost covered the glow from the ruby taped to her chest.

"Go back to bed, *chérie*," Lon said gently. "Kuttr here is very sorry for waking you, and he's going to officially and abjectly apologize at great length tomorrow morning when you're awake."

"Okay." She began to drag herself back to bed when Kuttr said, "Wait."

Lina turned at that, and Londo rose to take her arm to steer her to bed. "Sleep, Lina," he said giving Kuttr a nasty look before he returned his gaze to her.

"Heads up," Kuttr called, and both Londo and she turned to see three knives flashing at them, bulleting through the air. Lon reached out like lightning and caught them all even as Lina drew away from him with a gasp.

Kuttr watched her. Likely he was checking her reaction time. His eyes narrowed with calculation as his gaze dropped. Her robe was gaping, revealing that glow.

Londo returned the fire. Kuttr plucked the knives from the air with almost nonchalance, tucking them back into his tunic.

Lina stood there, fully waking, her knuckles white where she clutched her robe closed. This Kuttr man she'd seen at her wedding reception. He had won a Legion-wide bet about Londo's loss of virginity, and had been embarrassingly proud of it.

He was as short as she was, which would make him reasonably tall on Earth. His purple-tinged head was shaved long enough ago that it was now bristly. He was the very definition of "sinewy," in a lean way that would allow quick movement. "Is this what Legionnaires do when they have insomnia?" she finally demanded.

"*Chérie*," Londo urged as if nothing had happened. "Go back to bed. Kuttr's just trying to make a point. He's a terrible conversationalist."

Kuttr grunted. His gaze now moved to the blood on Londo's arm. She glanced at him suspiciously, her eyes sharp.

Kuttr watched as five knives of different widths appeared on the floor next to her. Then five smaller ones, six shuriken. His botha pellets, seifer coms, cok-kinsnaps, two-minuters, nat 'n' bones, climbing spikes... and his belt.

"I think I may have to strip him naked," she snapped at Londo, who'd assumed a crossed-arm stance as he watched the pile of weaponry on the rug grow. Boots and socks appeared next to the pile. "There are fibers in the clothes that don't really feel like they belong there. And all those little decorative patterns – they aren't just dec-orative. They do something, I don't know what."

"Leave him his modesty at least," Londo said in amusement. He himself stood there in his dark underwear.

"I don't think he has any."

"Quite right," Kuttr agreed, wiggling his bare toes. "It doesn't pay to be modest. And you missed some. Many things, actually. For instance..." He began calmly to peel back a false fingernail, and Lina drew back at the sight. "Duo-cat dots," he said as he picked something off the surface of the finger underneath.

"You attach them to a victim's skin," Londo explained to her, "and later you can expose them to an otherwise perfectly harmless gas. They'll be dead in thirty sec-onds."

"Lovely," Lina said, afraid that she might be sick. Here was someone who might actually use such a thing.

"He's used it," Londo assured her. "And he'll use it again."

Lina scanned him closer with her clairvoyance. In her imagination, blinking red arrows appeared to target things on Kuttr's body. Miniature demo videos seemed to run next to other items. Two angels shook their heads sadly at the need for the po-tential destruction they literally pointed out for her. "You have three of those fingernails, each with a dot under it," she reported. "Little prickly things between your toes – ow, that must hurt."

"One gets used to it," Kuttr said.

"There's a patch of false hair on... Oh, it's not just on your head." Lina blushed at that. "It looks like very thin plates of metal underneath. I don't get it."

"Mouth," Lon whispered at her behind his hand.

"Hm? Oh, there's a transmitter in a bicuspid. A number of tiny utensils in the molars. Permanent filters in your nose. A sorta click-down infrared sensing device under your eyelids..."

"Yuck. That's enough, *cherie*," Londo said. "No need to give yourself night-mares."

"No. I want to hear the entire list," Kuttr said.

"Okay. You've got a string on that last tooth, and it reaches down your throat for something. Some kind of tubing..." She tried to get a picture of what it did, and saw a mechanic using a snake light to peer at a hard-to-reach place. "What, some kind of light? Or sensing device?"

Kuttr made a noncommitted sound.

"A sparkling conversationalist," Londo commented.

"Let's see. Some kind of amps in your ears, and you control them by... by your thumb print?"

"It's a piece of magnetic latex," Kuttr said, as if that explained it.

"And an antenna up your ass," Lina finished. "Ew."

"Squeamishness can get you killed," Kuttr told her. "You missed a fair amount, but we'll call it a good inventory. Even though you did cheat." He pointed at the pile of weaponry. "Plus you managed to take out an entire arsenal by swiping my boots."

"But all in all, she got it," Londo said. "Lina, go to bed now."

"But–"

"I said, go to bed. It's bad enough that he woke you up." Londo put his arms around her. **I am not being a dictator on this. You need your sleep.**

She gave him a lazy smile. **Are you going to be here when I wake up?**

**That's why I want you to rest up now.**

"Well, okay. If you put it that way." She wrapped her arms around him as he leaned down for a warm kiss. "Don't be long; you need your rest, too," she said as she closed the door behind herself.


Londo watched her through the wall as she climbed into bed to make sure she really went, and then turned back to Kuttr to find him retrieving his weapons from the pile.

"How are her self-defense skills?" Kuttr asked.

"Non-existent."

Kuttr stopped at that. "But I thought she came from a primitive planet. Didn't she almost kill a Galactic Guard?"

"Just because Earth's a little behind the AffSys, doesn't mean that everyone walks around with a war 'bot mentality. She only got a good stranglehold on him. I saw the recording of it that the Ruby made. You would have had him dead three dozen times over with just one hand in the time she had. Unlike you, she's a pacifist. She had to crack through a few levels to get to the point where she was willing to kill."

"I suppose that might take a little time. Lessons."

"We've already told her that."

Kuttr's attention drew sharply to implications that had just occurred to him. "'We?' You and Jae?"

"Jae and I, yes."

"And you, too, Londo. Just in case those guides of hers don't come through."

"Don't even bother to throw it," Londo said quickly. "I'm completely invulnerable now."

"And telepathic too, it would seem," Kuttr said, considering the new circumstances. He slipped the shuriken back in place. "That could save your life, if you can detect a threat."

"It's already helped a number of times in that area."

"You'll need training on that, too."

"We have plans to go to Tishan. Eventually. We have a little deadline we want to make sure we meet first."

Kuttr nodded. "Understandable. But don't put it off longer than that, Londo, or you may regret it for the rest of your life. However short that may be." He looked up from refastening the Legion Array ankle band of his boot. "Get Jae to teach you a few moves. I hate to admit it—" He whirled around to catch two blades thrown at him from behind.

"Admit it," Jae said with a grin, standing in the entryway to the suite.

"I'll admit that you're better than Lon. Not better than me." Kuttr leisurely threw the blades back at Jae, who caught them and deposited them inside his tunic.

"And maybe I just don't have as big an ego as some people in this room." Jae walked to the end table to see if there was anything there for him. He came to one envelope and opened it, glancing at the formal script inside, and then set it back down. He looked up to Kuttr. "What, are you still here? Go away. Londo and I have to discuss some things. Three Worlds, not Legion."

"Is this the same business you spoke about with Lina last night?" Kuttr asked innocently.

Londo glanced at Jae and then at Kuttr. "What are you talking about?" he demanded, irritated.

"I put extra security on your room last night after I got in," Kuttr explained. "You three went in and a while later you came out, Londo. Jae didn't come out until morning."

"I was guarding Lina. Who was sleeping. You know that there have been attempts."

"Of course." Kuttr saw how Jae was standing behind Londo as he sat on the couch. Almost touching Londo, maybe his arm touched the very back of Londo's head. Jae wasn't looking at him. Quicker than thought, a knife flashed out of Kuttr's hand, heading towards Lon's forehead.

Lon's hand streaked out to catch the knife. "Dammit, Kuttr, when are you going to leave when you're told?"

"Apparently you can't give me the same bribe you gave your wife," Kuttr said with a smile as Lon flipped the knife back to him. He looked at it and pointedly wiped it on his tunic. A small smear of blood came off it. "Starhart," he said, "when you report for extra training, have Jae report with you. I think we'll be able to get truer responses with that combination." He paused. "We can turn off the surveillance cameras while we do it."

Jae put a steadying hand on Londo's shoulder. "Kuttr's been thinking too much lately," he said. "Thinking has never become you, Kuttr. It wakes up your brain. Gives you headaches."

"And occasionally gives me ideas."

"And just what ideas might you have had lately?" Londo asked, a growl in his voice.

Kuttr considered the two of them. "I've heard enough theories lately. About double-feedback telepathic loops and such. About how some things have to be taught. Thank the stars there's such a good teacher asleep in the next room."

Kuttr scratched the back of his neck. "You two have been best friends since you first met, haven't you? You've shared everything... except sexual preferences. Or am I wrong in that? What else have you shared?"

He watched them closely as both sets of eyes seemed to defocus ever so slightly. On top of it all, the two most powerful Legionnaires were now telepaths. A thrill of fear raced through him, quickly stanched.

"We share a disgust of people who can't keep their mouths shut about private matters, especially when they don't pertain to official Legion business. Things that they can't back up with evidence," Londo said quietly.

"Some might think this is evidence enough," Kuttr said, fingering the bloody patch where he'd wiped his blade.

Lon didn't like that blood. He hated to think it, but… There would have to be consideration made for his new condition. And here was someone else who knew at least part of their secret.

"Kuttr doesn't make accusations," Jae told Lon.

"He isn't a good conversationalist at that," Lon agreed sullenly.

"But I do enjoy hearing a good confession," Kuttr said. "If I can get the two of you in my dojo, you'll soon be begging me to hear what you have to say."

"What a blowhard."

"C'mon, Jae," Londo said, patting his husband on the arm and rising from the couch. He let his hand slide down Jae's arm to intertwine his fingers with his. "Let's get to bed. Good night, Kuttr. Feel free to guard the suite. From the outside."

Kuttr laughed as they closed the door behind him, locking it.

# 14

Kuttr trooped down the hallway after the next shift change even as Wiley approached from the opposite direction. Wiley paused but Kuttr didn't, striding purposefully toward the Starhart suite. They arrived at the door at the same time and regarded each other even as the Legionnaire assigned to guard the room stood aside for them.

"I have been informed that I have an apology to make to the lady," Kuttr said. Both Wilder's eyes settled their independent movement to focus on the shorter Legionnaire without saying anything, and he buzzed the room.

"In," they heard Londo's voice say, and entered.

Lon and Lina were seated at a breakfast table in their robes. Londo had a cell phone to his ear. "We have visitors, Hal," he told it. "Talk to you later." He put down the phone and cocked his head at the newcomers.

"If we're going to be having company, Londo," Lina told him, "I need to be getting ready for the day. I've got to move us all soon."

"No. No move today. We cancelled it. No more moves."

Lina squinted her eyes, trying to capture the memory. "We did? We did. Oh good. Anyway, this isn't exactly what Miss Manners would approve of. Or Legion Protocol. They're probably handing me demerits right now."

"It's just family," Lon said, squeezing her hand. "No need to stand on formality."

Kuttr bowed to Lina. "If it would make you feel more comfortable, you may strip me again. Just like last night," he added for Wiley's benefit.

"You were supposed to be getting some natural sleep, and you're throwing orgies instead," Wiley accused Lina.

"It was my fault," Kuttr said, "and I apologize. I thought it was a good time to test some theories I had that you hadn't entirely made public." Kuttr then glared at

Wiley. "Sometimes it's good to get your nose out of your ass and face real potentials."

"I suppose you're talking about Londo's vulnerability problems," Wiley replied huffily. "I have taken–"

"Morning, everyone!" Jae entered the room from the second bedroom in the suite, a direction that took Kuttr by surprise. Jae was fully dressed in uniform, unlike his spouses. "A party, and no one told me." He crossed to the table and bent down to kiss Londo on the mouth. "Morning, love," he said, giving his neck a quick but soft caress. He kissed Lina, too. "Morning, sweet. Don't tell me you got old blood 'n guts to order an entirely vegetarian meal?"

Lina smiled as Londo pulled Jae down into a chair. "This world doesn't domesticate animals for food," he said.

"A very civilized place," Lina approved. She settled back to watch the boys and their mind games, noting that Wiley was a bit startled by the gay interplay, and Kuttr's eyebrows had almost arched off his forehead entirely. There was a difference between intellectual knowledge and having reality slap you in the face. She had to grin quickly into her plate.

"How many other people know?" Kuttr finally said. "Maximus?"

"No," Lon said too quickly.

"That's a mistake. How many are going to find out when you've been as sloppy as you have? Jae, they use a cleaning service here, not kol-vanaschen. Someone's bound to notice that your quarters haven't been slept in. And that the other bedroom here was."

"No one will notice anything. The room here is cleaner than it was when we arrived. And the room allotted to me has indeed been slept and lived in. Or so it would appear."

"You did visit your room last night, but only for about ten minutes each time."

"You're a nosy bastard, Kuttr."

Lina said, "He seems to be helping. A bit. We're being more careful." She looked at the outer door. "Stoan's coming," she said. "I'm going to go get dressed."

"Stay here," Londo said. "If you and I match, it will help the image."

"You should tell him," Wiley said.

"They shouldn't," Kuttr said. "Open marriage is definitely not approved protocol."

"It's not an open marriage," Londo began when the door buzzed.

"In," Jae called out. The door opened immediately, and Stoan looked a little startled at the crowd.

"Who's eaten and who hasn't?" Jae asked around the table. "I'm starved. Let me call for more breakfast."

"Get something for me, then," Kuttr said.

"Me too," Wiley said as he reached into his pocket for a notepadd. He opened it slightly, just enough that a sliver of screen was visible, and brought up a definition for the words *Feithi Triune*, showing the screen surreptitiously to Kuttr. Kuttr's right eyebrow didn't raise, although it quivered as if it wanted to. Stoan didn't notice.

"Stoan?"

"*Nacchin*," Stoan said. "A very informal meeting going on here, I see."

"I am getting dressed," Lina murmured.

Lon caught her arm.

"No, really, love. I'll feel more comfortable," she told him.

"Your breakfast will get cold."

"So you warm it up for me when I get back," she said with a smile and a squeeze.

When she returned, weaving the final ribbons into her braid, the men were all still around the table drinking from giant mugs of nacchin, a bitter drink that Lina had tried and dismissed a few days ago. Someone had opened one of those holographic communication deals with Andri, so she sat at table level with the group as if she were actually there. The only thing different about her presence was that the transmitting padd cropped her image abruptly where it met its folded edge.

They all were discussing Legionnaire schedules and which seminar delegations still hadn't arrived at their planet. The final class of the final day of the Tour would be a crowded one to hold the latecomers, which meant it would last longer than normal.

Lina sat down to her plate and Londo blew on it, heating it up. She saw a new service cart and steaming fare that must have just arrived. This planet really did use people as waiters and not machinery or replicators in the rooms. She frowned at the platters.

"I don't want any more stunts like you pulled with that artificial telepath, Carolina," Stoan glared at her. "No taking chances on anything, not until all of this is through."

She smiled sweetly at him. "Why don't you try some of the orange stuff there?" She pointed at the central platter on the service cart. Her guides were pointing madly at it and making "stay away!" gestures. "I hear it's delicious." She turned to Wiley. "All these tests are really getting tiresome. When do they end?"

It was Kuttr who answered. "When life ends," he said. "Life is a series of tests. I make it a matter of habit to scan any food that I myself have not prepared, even if it's replicated. Scan the air, scan the water, scan the walls…"

"Maybe it's not necessary to be that thorough all the time," Jae told Lina, "but you should get into the habit of checking out food as well as rooms. Especially when you're in a strange place."

"That's true," Andri chimed in. Within her screen she was eating a sandwich wrap. Its savory aroma added to that of the breakfast in the room.

"This wasn't your doing," Lina nodded at the food but meant Stoan.

"Someone on this planet doesn't like somebody or somebodies in this room," Londo said. "A slow-acting poison. Relatively slow; it would take about an hour to take effect."

Lina shuddered. Poison! Again!

Kuttr leaned back in his chair. "And just think – if your husband there–" and his eyes glanced quickly to Jae, as opposed to the husband *there* "–were to be holding your hand as he was eating, it would affect him just as thoroughly as you. Check your food. Check your environment. Check the people around you."

Jae stood and bowed his head over the platter. Lina could feel him talking internally to the food and the devas of its chemical structure. Then he brought the dish back to the table with him and began to eat directly from it. Stoan frowned at him but allowed it; he knew that the poison was now neutralized.

Lina pushed her plate away. "I can't be in contact with my guides all the time," she tried to explain. "They're on a higher vibration than we are, way higher than even Jae."

Wiley took note of that. So did Andri.

"If I were to try, if it didn't tire me out completely, I'd go over the edge. I'd go crazy. My mind wouldn't be in synch with the material world."

Stoan started to make a crack and reconsidered.

"Your brain would soon re-synchronize with reality," Wiley postulated.

"I read a book once," Lina said, "about a near-death survivor who was also a brain surgeon. He thought that the human brain actually dumbs down the real universe, filters it, so we can work with it on material levels."

"Hunh." Wiley slowly chewed that over even as he chewed some tuddlies.

"I'll get you that book," Lina promised as she decided she was still hungry after all. "Remind me." She reached over to Jae's plate to spear food from where he hadn't yet sampled.

Londo spoke up. "Legionnaires have access to sensors that constantly check for known poisons and catalysts in the immediate vicinity. I want Lina to be issued one, permanently."

Stoan thought for a moment and nodded. "Considering the number of assassination attempts already – approved."

"I'll notify Logistics," Andri said.

Wiley held up a ringed finger. "I think I can handle that. I'll configure her earring for environmental threats."

"Makes my job easier," Andri replied with a smile at him.

He smiled back.

Lina perked up at Stoan's information. It sounded like more than the two attempts she knew of that the Tour had encountered. Jeez. "What number would that be?"

"You still keep your antenna up," Londo told her sternly.

"Just as long as I don't have to keep my antenna where Kuttr keeps his," Lina rolled her eyes at her husband, and Londo laughed.


First Lina checked on the three Aldierran women. It had been long enough for the rescued women to have had a thorough rest. Though it was early for Lina's work day, planet-time they were well into afternoon. The women were looking much better, their skin flushing a healthier orange than before. Was it her imagination, or were they coughing less?

They'd been with psychotherapists a few hours already. Mart had been replaced by Dr. Benton from Legion Medical, the woman who was the secondary doctor for the Tour. Daisley, Lon's team medic, was partnering with Benton for the ladies. The efficient, blue-skinned medic was working on notes and trying not to intrude on the current conversation.

Dawn now wore a patch over her wounded nose, something that was molded and colored to look like a normal nose so that you barely noticed it. Daisley had offered her corrective surgery, but she'd declined. She was even unsure about the prosthetic. She complained that it made her look pretty.

Lina told her that decision was fine and they could get her an uglier prosthetic if she wanted. If after a while she decided for the surgery, Lina would arrange it.

Lina had no idea how they'd afford all this, but somehow she'd see it done.

The women told her about what they knew of the state of womanhood on their planet. Andri joined them in the all-female room, not commenting often. She represented the Legion, which was an official AffSys organization, and the AffSys government was keen to find out everything it could about the previously unknown planet that had dared wage war upon their capital planet.

These women hadn't been exposed to a world beyond their community. They'd been kept in compounds that were populated by a very extended family, going back six generations if not more. The compounds, or just plain *Houses* were differentiated from others in name by colors and patterns, character traits and sometimes seemingly normal, random titles, and were small villages within their larger towns and cities.

Women were uneducated. They could count, but not to high numbers. They couldn't read. They listened to news but didn't know geography or politics enough to make much sense of it.

But they knew how to cast spells and curses. Sometimes those worked; sometimes they didn't. Plus, they had their grandmothers' cures for illnesses, which also sometimes worked. This was a good thing, since they had no access to medical services. Women were noted for their short lifespans.

Their only duties were to provide sex for the men, sons for their houses, and 24/7 intensive servant service.

"We will institute women's shelters where they can go if they feel unsafe," Lina told them.

"That would be every woman in the world," Hope said.

"Then it will be for every woman in the world." Despite not knowing where the money for such would come from, Lina's voice held steel in it, and the women's eyes widened. "We *will* do this somehow. There will be counseling. I think everyone, including the men, need it. The world seems to be suffering from severe mental illness and trauma at many levels. We can't allow this to go on, to pollute further generations.

"Lon sometimes uses a virtual therapist," she continued, "a computer version of his real one, and he says that works well. With something like that we could possibly reach everyone fairly quickly. We'll look into it."

"Speaker," Dawn responded reverently as she bowed her head.

Hope had also bowed her head, but now raised it slightly and squinted at Lina out of one eye. "Is there a way for the world to kill only the men? We women are not responsible for the troubles. Only the men."

"Kill the men." Spring nodded vigorously.

Lina rubbed her mouth. The visions returned: Granger over her. Granger doing the terrible things he did to Demi. These women had similar experiences, and such seemed everyday occurrences. "We will try our best to change the men," she finally decided to say. "All of them. They probably mistreat some of their own, don't they? The weaker ones."

"Younger. The sick. The weak," Hope said.

"Only a few of them are hurt. It's *all* of *us* that suffer," Spring said.

"Okay. We're going to try to dig out the rot, but we need women to help us." Lina had no idea if she was saying the right thing or not. "I don't know how Aldierra will carry out whatever it is she'll do. But we're going to give our best effort into seeing it doesn't happen. Everyone. Men and women of Aldierra, together. Maybe this working together will help bring change about."

The women looked doubtful.

"We will educate women. You do have access to broadcasts?" At their nods, Lina nodded as well. "Virtual classes for everyone, especially the women. Jae's finishing up the arrangements for our communications network right now; we just need non-military personnel to staff it. I'm hoping to get AffSys help on it as well." She looked at Andri, who nodded. Good.

"We'll create medical facilities, specifically for females and run by females. Maybe we can get some AffSys medical colleges to offer residencies on Aldierra, do you think, Andri? Is AffSys virtual medicine any good? It's going to take a lot of time to reach everyone. Twenty billion people… That would be about five billion females.

"How about birth control?" Lina asked the trio.

The women looked confused and then as they comprehended the term, they gawped at her.

Andri nudged Lina to whisper, "This is really a thing?" She'd never had to worry about such.

"It is a super-major thing," Lina said before turning back to the women. "Safe abortion? Obstetrics? Neo-natal care? Help for new mothers?

"How are the handicapped treated on your world? Both men and women? What's childcare like?"

The discussions went on, and Andri's aide as well as Lina's earring noted it all for others to study, as well as added to the Aldierran lexicon for the translators.

As the ladies seemed to be tiring, Andri had her staff direct them to a hyperspace ship. They were going to Sarastor. Andri had agreed to put them up in Legion guest quarters because she wanted their visitors monitored and recorded. There they'd receive further medical attention as well as be able to access luxury treatments they'd never dreamed of, but would also meet with architects and sociologists Londo and Jae had lined up. They'd help design the women's shelters to fit Aldierran standards.

Thankfully the Affiliated Systems had little experience in the problem of battered women. Between Lina and her Tour cohorts though, Terran experts with practical experience in the problem of battered women and sheltering the same were contacted. Ships were sent to transport them as well, which meant the ParaNet had to be alerted to the interstellar visitors. Jae arranged for the experts to have Sarastoran guides who would also monitor and aid them as needed.

In a few days there'd be a plan for establishing a network of women's shelters across Aldierra. They all kept in mind that these women were unworldly, and that needs would surely vary across the planet's landscape and sub-cultures. But this would be a start.

In addition to her husbands, Lina needed to talk with Aldierra's leaders. The Aldierrans were calling their deadline "Doomsday." This seemed like they didn't have high hopes for achieving anything, and thus wouldn't strive for anything to achieve.

The three of them needed to change that attitude, pronto.

Good thing the final day of the Tour was fast approaching. Get the classes over with, and perhaps they should re-think taking a day off afterward. Get right on the Aldierran crisis full time.

After all, they had access to stims.


The initial brightness of being that had accompanied the stims that began the day was dulled by the time the entire staff took a long lunch break after the first class at the secured restaurant they'd previously visited. Legion Security attended in force, with an additional multitude of Legionnaires guarding the place and a few more eating around the room.

The staff was heartily tired of eating in the tiny, secured restaurants the hotels had provided. There the food was labelled "nutritious," with no notation of whether it tasted good or not. Here there was actual enjoyable food. The puzzle was to discover which dishes that applied to.

Lina was bleary because Dr. Mart had given her minimal stims for the occasion. A short lunch and long nap were what he recommended instead for the Tour staff. Especially her, despite her schedule. Mart was beginning to disapprove of stims as a regular diet.

Both Lon and Jae had adjusted their schedules to allow them to attend as well as cover Aldierra business afterward. Enough people shared the Starharts' table that no little touches between the spouses could be allowed. Sue Taylor chatted with her friend Dinah and the Tishana Mar-yo, all now quite comfortable with being in the presence of heroes.

It was early morning local time. Those window screens showed a brightening purple-pink sky with high clouds blown by the crisp winds that made it too cool to go out and grab a lungful of unfiltered air. Some of the world's moons showed faintly through the daylight.

In a sweeping plaza, people hurried by a crowd in coats with high Elvis collars gathered tightly around them. Capes flapped behind them in addition to the coats. The men had bare legs while women wore fuzzy tights.

That crowd was growing. "What is it?" Lina asked as outside sound began to whisper into the restaurant. The plaza must be close if they could hear things through the walls.

Londo cocked his head and listened for a moment, then spotted Mimik sitting nearby. He did something to his Legion ring and Mimik glanced over at their table, gave Londo a nod, and left.

Eight minutes later she returned to draw up a chair next to Lon. She spoke low but Lina could hear her clicking words. "It's a political rally. They're saying we're practicing or teaching Mind Control. Different people are voicing similar ideas. The gist is that we're enabling a diabolical planetary coup."

Londo nodded and then glanced around the restaurant. All the Tour assistants were there. Stoan sat across the room, present informally as part of the Legion's security force.

"Commander, could you come over here?" Lon asked through his ring.

Stoan did so and leaned over the table next to Londo. "What's up?"

"The crowd." Lon nodded to the direction of outside the window. "An outside force must be egging them on. They're bound to cause trouble. I was wondering if you could calm them down."

"Do the All-Powerful Legion Commander routine?" Stoan studied the throng thoughtfully. "Are they that much of a danger, do you think?" He glanced at Mimik as well as Lon and Jae for their opinion. "The Tour's gone on long enough now that I wouldn't expect anything big."

"I think. Jae?"

Jae turned to them and nodded, his face tight. "Erik says someone out there is really stirring them up. It could be Imperials. I heard Rikli was in town."

Londo tensed at the name.

"The emperor certainly has enough contacts on this planet," Stoan said quietly. "He or his underlings could coordinate this with no problem. We're too damn close to the Empire here." Stoan had no love lost to the emperor either. He'd seen too many debacles that could be linked back to Yanist-Glory, and Londo was a good friend, his macabre childhood history well-known to him.

Sue Taylor glanced from Londo to this blue-clad, blue-skinned para whom everyone deferred to. They both looked deadly serious. "*They* say if you're going to speak to the crowd, the sooner the better," she told Londo.

"They say?" Stoan asked her. His face suddenly took on understanding. "Oh no. Not–"

"Guides," Londo said with a little smile.

"Do all Terrans–?"

"No," Londo answered. "Sue is the original teacher for this psychic group. There was a class a handful of years ago."

Sue nodded at Stoan. "*They* say you wield a lot of influence, that the people – the ones who are being manipulated, not the ones behind this – will listen to you. But if you wait too long a mob mentality will take over, and there's no way to talk your way through that."

Beside her Dinah nodded in agreement.

"Londo, you have to talk too," Lina said quietly. "At least let yourself be seen." She had already noticed how he was as well-known here as Maximus. Two voices of reason would calm the fears even more.

"Who's behind this?" Jae asked Lina.

Her eyes unfocused. "Just one person. A man. He's got… an attitude around him. Of power. Of entitlement. I assume it's the emperor, but Lon's stories may have influenced me. I see him sitting in a red room on a red-upholstered chair with... with slaves in shackles lying at his feet, worlds in shackles lying at his feet... The sound of people without hope groaning all around him..."

"That's Yanist-Glory," Londo said, linking with her. "I'll show you photos later."

Lina nodded. "I'll keep a watch out for him," she said. She turned to the crowd. "Ah. There are people out there who work for him, or are associated with him somehow. There are invisible chains surrounding the plaza."

Jae said, "We could have them detained. That way they'd stop instigating the mob."

"And it could blow up in our face," Stoan pointed out. "The crowd might see it as an attack against them, to take away their leaders."

Londo said, "So talk to them, Stoan. I'll stand next to you and do my Maximus impression."

Lina turned to him with a questioning smile on her face.

Jae nudged her. "You have to have seen it, Lina. He crosses his arms in front of himself and scowls."

"I thought that was just him being Valiant," Lina said.

"With this the feet are wider apart and he tilts his head to his right." Mimik added, "The right eyebrow is also cocked. An excellent re-creation."

Jae nodded in agreement. "It *is* very impressive."

Lina giggled a little. "Does Hal know he's doing him?"

Jae grinned. "He has no idea in this world. Or any other."

"It's effective," Lon said to the both of them. "It scares the shit out of people."

Lina couldn't imagine anything being more frightening than Lon in his Warrior mode. He did look up to his adoptive father so.

Stoan straightened up. "All right, Londo. I'll do my Legion Commander impression, you do your Maximus impression, and let's get rid of this mob."

Londo moved to follow him as they left the restaurant.

"Lina, I want you to point out the Glory supporters to me," Jae said. "Behind cover. Let's get some local police with us so they can keep track of them too."

# 15

S ue and some others from the Tour joined them as they trailed Stoan and Londo. They descended a few stories to utilize a balcony that was just above the crowd. Jae coordinated with the officers to construct a low-grade forcefield around the Tour participants, with gaps in the wavelength so they could peek outside but still remain under cover.

Aides quickly set up broadcasting equipment. Within minutes amplifiers and a universal-view video screen hovered over the plaza.

Stoan spoke into his ring. "Any Legionnaires not directly guarding Tour partici-pants, police the plaza and environs outside." Then he stepped to the front of the balcony where people below could easily see him.

With a crook of the fingers of his left hand, a subliminal, eye-catching multicol-ored light began to play upon him. "You know who I am," Stoan told the crowd with the ease and confidence of someone who often spoke before large groups. "You all know Valiant here, and Neutrino from the Legion. There are more Legionnaires in-side, protecting the people who are giving and attending these sessions, so you don't have to be afraid of anyone trying to influence the event."

"Over there," Lina quietly told one officer. "These people are spread out, not together. That one's in a white coat by the little post."

"There and there." Sue pointed and tried to describe the exact location.

One of the Tishana had brought a padd that linked into some monitoring camera system. "Here," Meb said, pointing to the person on screen.

"And this one. I think. Not sure." Sweeney gave her own ideas to the officer nearest her.

"The Legion's taking over the planet!" someone in the crowd yelled, using an amplifier of their own.

"That's idiotic," Stoan scowled. "The Legion is not interested in staging coups. We have evidence that Yanist-Glory is trying to get his foot in the door on your world. We're here to stop that, to make sure that your government remains in your hands, not his."

"Legion off of Traim! Legion off of Traim!"

"You can guess who signs their pay credits," Stoan told the crowd, who stirred uncomfortably as they realized that they weren't sure whose motives were what. "Let me tell you again: the Legion is here to oversee the seminars to protect those who attend and those who are giving them. The seminars are being held so that we will never again fear Mind Control. This is something we can now detect… and *cure*. The controlled can return to their normal state of mind. I've seen it done."

He didn't mention that it had been done to him. "For years Yanist-Glory has used Mind Control to bring new worlds under his sway. Now his people, the spies whom he has in his employ on this world, are nervous. They know that they won't be able to overthrow your government if they can't control key personnel. They're scared, so they're trying to mislead you into thinking that we or someone else is out to take over. This isn't true."

He glanced at Londo, and the microphone floated over to him. "Yanist-Glory can't rely on Mind Control anymore," Lon told the crowd, "but there are other ways of controlling people – like using fear, distrust, and conspiracy theories. Stirring up a mob, making people think something's going on when it's not. I personally have de-controlled people. It's easy. Anyone can do it, anyone can learn. That's what the Tour participants are doing here today. They have learned how to do it and are now taking that knowledge home with them to teach others, who will teach even more."

Lina and the others' conversations with officers behind him continued quietly.

"Yeah, there's one," Lina said, nodding and not pointing in case the person could see her through the forcefield gap. "The man in the yellow cape and brown coat. With the red thing on the top of his head." If she looked just beyond reality, she could see the handful of exclamation marks hovering over people in the crowd. It was an effective symbol, and Lina thanked her guides for it.

"Got him," the officer said, nodding to one of his companions, who quickly exited along with others.

"And that woman over there, looking around. Green coat behind that little group of everyone in beige. She's realizing that something's up." The woman edged toward the outside of the crowd, moving to leave the area.

"We'll follow her," the officer assured Lina. She shivered in the cold and tried to keep her mind on what she was doing. Fatigue was blurring her perceptions. Her stims were wearing off.

She could hear her staff murmuring to their officers. But… But…

"Something's going to happen," Lina blurted. "A divers–" They saw a flash from the street that edged the plaza. A ground vehicle flipped up in the air, spinning around as it arced even as the sound of the explosion reached them. Lon sped to it. He grabbed it while it was still in mid-air, before it could land on top of a knot of people retreating from the mob.

Jae saw that there were injured from the blast. "That's it. Everyone inside. Hurry. You too, Lina," he told her. He flew off to help in the plaza.

Lina nodded and herded her people out, but hesitated when the door loomed in front of her. She came to a full stop, trying to taste what it was. "There's something else," she mumbled to herself. What was it?

"Some kind of… Kind of…" Lina ported back to the force field and peered out a crack. "What the heck is it?"

"What are you doing here?" Stoan demanded from behind her. "Get inside. Now."

"There are three exclamation marks," she told him. "Not one. Three. Over the same person. It's something… big."


Stoan began to argue with her, but instead he peered out the same crack. "We have people scanning for weaponry. Nothing there out of the ordinary."

Lina cocked her head. "The exclamation points are going all wonky. Crazy fonts. I think *they're* trying to tell me that this is out of the ordinary. Ouch! They shocked me, like I'd stuck my finger into a power outlet. What don't you normally scan for? It's electric. You should scan for electric."

Stoan frowned as he used his electromagnetic senses to search for…

"He's pretty confident about it," Lina said. "Don't know if it's a he or a she, but… confidence. No, determination. Brutality."

There. There was a nexus of magnetism over there. Stoan edged in front of Lina. "Get behind me. I've got him."

"What the heck is it? He's reaching for it. On his back, pulling it forward. It's a rifle, but not a rifle. It… it… Damned technology! It has something to do with… the body's electricity?"

"Yeaaah. That's a bio-shocker all right," Stoan said almost to himself as he felt the familiar power inflow in that area. A particularly nasty weapon used by fanatics. He'd only run into them a handful of times. After a few shots of that, there wasn't much life left in the shooter. He touched his ring. "Bioshocker," he warned his people. "Evacuate the plaza asap!"

To his senses, the nexus began to turn a bright blue and pulled at his own electromagnetism.

"Final charge-up!" Stoan moved to point toward the assassin, focusing his own powers. "Get down!" he ordered Lina as the gun fired.

He was too late to stop it, but he could bend the world's magnetic lines of force. That disrupted the shot, weakened it and twisted it off-target. It crashed against the side of the building, just above Lina. Stoan threw up a magnetic shell around her, adding to the force field in front of her. A small portico along the building shattered. Metal fragments rained outside a circle around the two of them.

She ported to his other side. "Another. There's another. Maybe two?" she said quickly. "No, just one more."

Stoan sent a blast of magnetism toward the would-be assassin, pinning him to the ground with his own harnessed bio-electricity. "Where?"

"I don't know!" Her unfocused eyes darted back and forth, as telepaths' did when they were using their abilities. "*They* say you can see them if you look.

"I see a bird," she continued. "I see a camera. I… Bird's eye view?" Her face contorted into a frown of concentration. "Are they up somewhere? Not down in the plaza, but–"

"Up there." Stoan growled as he spotted the shooter on the rooftop. "He hasn't charged yet," Stoan confirmed as he saw Lina look where he was looking. "Port me," he ordered, and he was there in an instant. He stood behind the armed woman, who aimed the clear plastic of the barrel that ran down the length of her arm. Stoan put his hand on the woman's shoulder and scrambled every neuron she had. The assassin arced back as if she'd had an epileptic seizure and fell unconscious to the ground.

"The first one is recharging. Port me to him," Stoan said to the air, hoping that Lina could hear him.

Instantly he was there, where the would-be assassin hadn't had time to recover though he hadn't been captured. Instead of trying to escape, he'd begun the charge cycle. Stoan fried the man's nervous system but with less force than he'd done for his cohort. He was already a third or so of the way to being dead after that first shot.

Stoan looked up at the balcony where he'd been standing. He couldn't see Lina, but now he could hear music. He leapt into the air and kept going as his Legion Array took over, flying him to the balcony.

She sat in lotus position looking as calm as if she'd been somewhere alone, just playing for herself. The flute music drifted lazily on the air, rolling over the crowd. They quieted as they heard it, the red haze of panic leaving their eyes. Beginning to look around to see where friends were, to stop and see what was going on instead of relying on their fear to tell them to run.

Stoan reached for his microphone. "It would be a good idea if everyone left," he told the crowd quietly. "We've managed to catch a few of Yanist-Glory's assassins and spies. Go home. Think for yourselves." He stood there stoically as the crowd meandered into slow streams out and away from the plaza.

He kept magnetic shields in place around the two assassins until the plaza cleared out. Then he lifted the one on the building roof and drew her along the planet's lines of force to join her associate on the ground. Both of them twitched as Legionnaires gathered to secure their weapons. A long ambulance had already come for the victims of the blast. More arrived for these criminals.

The music stopped. Lina stood next to Stoan, surveying the scene. She watched the activity on the street, however, where Jae and Londo both were helping the crowd evacuate. She nodded in their direction as if engaged in a silent conversation, and then turned around to check the building where the blast had been. There was now a sizable hole in the wall that revealed the metal structure of the building, as well as optical wiring and insulation. Something that was not water slowly dripped from the hole.

"Thank you," she told Stoan without looking at him. He didn't say anything. She brushed building dust from herself, non-metallic material that Stoan's shield hadn't protected her from. "I'll have to take another shower before class," she said miserably and stopped. "Oh."

It was the way she said it that caught his attention. "What?" he demanded.

"There's someone in our room," she said. "He's got one of those guns, charged. No, it's not a gun. It's... It's the same kind of idea, though. But you don't aim it."

"Bio-bomb," Stoan said grimly. Worse than a bio-shocker. Everything in one suicide blast. "Listen to me. When I give the word, you're going to port him out here, mid-air, higher than the buildings, above the center of the plaza."

"But he'll..."

"He's dead already. If he's charged the bomb, he's already committed suicide. I'll alert Londo to stand by." Stoan motioned to an officer inside the building and they conferred for a moment. The officer nodded grimly.

Stoan turned to her. "Do it," he said, and glanced up.

The man appeared there, held shakily in position no doubt by her levitation. But almost as soon as he materialized, he exploded into tiny pieces of shrapnel and blood.

Lina let out a clipped shriek.

A directed wind blew it all together, kept it from scattering over the landscape, over them. Londo flashed back and forth, blowing it all back into itself until the protoplasm that used to be a man plopped onto the pavement of the plaza as a pile. Londo disappeared for a few minutes. Stoan had an idea that he was off being sick to his stomach somewhere. He thought that if Lina weren't here, he'd be doing the same thing.

Erik appeared from down a street, flying in even as a more general wind rose. Under his control it began to circulate, finding the finer particles of the blast that were still floating, and funneling them to the pile.

"I… I think…" Lina said in a shaky voice. "I th-think someone needs to tell the organizers that we'll be starting later than we'd planned." She disappeared.

"*Kicking skurn!*" Stoan exclaimed. He twisted the symbol of his ring. "Londo! That wife of yours just ported out without a guard! I think she went back to your room."

Lon's voice sounded wan. "I'll get her. Thanks, Stoan."

Lon almost ran through the shower. The remaining protoplasm particles sluiced down the drain. ****I'm coming!**** He scrubbed the vomit out of his mouth– ****I'm here, cherie, I'm here!**–** and threw a towel around himself. When he emerged into their bedroom, Lina was sitting on the edge of the bed, shaking. She'd covered her face with her hands.

All Lina could see was the smoke and laser fire and terror that had been the corridors under the Rimhold prison weeks ago. Shouting. Explosive blasts. Bodies in the dimness. Blood. The groans of the dying. And her desperately trying not to be one of them, even as the prison guards levelled their weapons at her.

Now… a body blowing up within the chaos, disintegrating into blobs.

The sound she emitted was something between a sob and a whine of distress.

Londo folded her into his arms. "I'm here," he kept repeating. "Breathe. Breathe."

Jae slammed open the outer door and rushed in. His right cheek had been scorched. Ash and grime covered his body except for a hand mark on his left boot. His cape was shredded on the side.

Lina looked up to see him. "Oh no, Jae," she moaned and tried to stand. Lon eased her back down.

"Jae's going to take a shower," he told Lina even as he directed him toward the bathroom and its shower with a sharp jerk of his chin. Jae nodded and obeyed.

"We'll call a doctor for him when he gets out," Lon assured her. "It looks worse than it likely is."

Lina rubbed her forehead miserably against his bare chest. "And you. Oh, Londo! What you had to– Awful. Awful!"

"Yes, yes. And my therapist is going to hear all about it at our next appointment." He lifted her chin with a finger so she would look at his face. "I'm fine. Jae will be fine. I've seen him much worse and he turned out fine. Now let's talk about you. Therapist."

Her mouth worked soundlessly as her eyes looked this way and that, searching for a way out. "I, I guess," she finally decided.

"I heard you the other day. You said our therapists were great. Did great work. Now tell me: do you ever take your own advice?"

The smallest of smiles came to her. "Maybe not."

He rubbed her back and kissed her forehead. "*Chérie, chérie.*"

"I don't know…"

"Don't make me… No, I won't order you. But I *will* trick you into doing it."

Jae emerged from the bathroom, similarly wrapped as Londo, but he scrubbed a towel over his hair. He avoided brushing his cheek with it, as well as his right side.

"Oh, Jae!" Lina exclaimed. Londo would not let her up. However, he did slide away so Jae could take his turn at hugging comfort into his wife.

Lon touched his ring as he pulled up an ottoman so he could position himself on Lina's other side. "Mart to the Starharts' room," he directed. "Unless you have serious injuries to attend to. In that case… Daisley to the Starharts' room. Not an emergency." In an aside, he told Lina, "Daisley's my team medic, remember? They both can keep secrets."

"Oof!" Lina exclaimed as a timed stim kicked in. "I guess it's time for class. I'm not going until Jae's seen to."

Jae touched his cheek and grimaced. "It's not bad. Just needs a small fix-up." He then touched his own ring. "Neutrino to Tour personnel: We're going to take…" He motioned and a screen appeared in front of him with the class schedule. "Another forty-five minutes before team members need to report. Tell everyone." To his spouses he said, "We'll attend to Aldierra after class."

Daisley was the first to arrive. Her eyes opened wide as she took in the scene of two Legionnaires, one of them her Team Leader, sitting in only towels with Lina Starhart between them.

"Jae first," Londo instructed the doctor and released Lina. "You get cleaned up."

At first she stumbled when she got up, but her steps became less wobbly as she made her way to the bathroom. "I'll find a new outfit while you're in there," Lon called behind her.

Lon fussed over Jae as the doctor saw to him. He stroked the hair on the uninjured side of Jae's head. "Love, try to avoid the line of fire," he advised.

Daisley pressed her lips together.

"It's all right; we're married," Lon blithely said even as he tried to catch every detail of her reaction. He needed this kind of data to determine when he could announce. What would people think of him? Would they reject him, even his closest friends?

"Married." Daisley looked from him to Jae, who batted his eyes at her, over an endearing smile that twitched as his cheek protested. "Need to know?"

"For now, yes." It was a Legion way of saying that things were secret. "A Feithi Triune."

"I will have to look that one up. Later." Daisley attended to Jae's other injuries, which were annoying and a bit painful, but slight as Legion injuries went.

Thus Jae was all patched up when Mart reported in.

"Ah, excellent," Jae said before Lon could say anything. "I'm fine; Lon is fine, but we need to have you research therapists for our wife. She has finally decided to accept help in that area."

Lon had suspected Jae would say something so he shrugged. "She'll try to get out of it."

Mart's mouth moved from side to side.

"Feithi Triune," Daisley said helpfully as she repacked her med kit.

"Well," Mart said. Clearing his throat gave him time to take it all in. "Well. I was wondering if this would come up. The stims can't have helped PTSD. Though come to think of it, they may have insulated her mind against the trauma. Once she comes off the stims, she might find herself overwhelmed."

"I suggest keeping her on minimum doses until she can be monitored," Daisley said. "There's not much research on massive stim use."

"We can certainly add our data to the base." Mart frowned. Jae pulled on boots over his tights, his expression barely masking a grimace of pain. "Very well. When shall I schedule?"

Lina walked out of the bathroom. She was dressed for the Tour, with ribbons in her hair. It was still wet, so she wore it down where it could dry naturally. "After the Tour," she told the doctors. "I can handle it until then. We'll have time the day after the Tour ends, before we begin full on Aldierra. There won't be time afterward."

She turned to her husbands. "How long does it take? Is it *boom*, they give me a pill or a shot?"

Lon knew that Lina would have seen Jae sometimes touch his inner forearm to release meds. They controlled his manic problem.

"It is not," Jae assured her. "I've been in therapy since... Since, you know." The death of Feith and all its people.

"But I don't have all that to deal with. I can handle this. I mean, I feel much better."

Jae and Lon rolled their eyes at each other. Mart and Daisley did the same.

Lon pointed that commanding index finger of his at Lina. "You're a Starhart now."

Jae chuckled. "Everyone knows that Starharts are, what's the phrase, Lon? *Looney Tunes.* We need our therapy, at least once a week."

"Apply more often as needed." Lon nodded. "Therapy makes the Starharts sane."

"I don't think my cats would recognize me if I were entirely sane." Lina sighed. "Starharts together.

"I can make it until the end of the Tour. I'll just remember to breathe deeply. Meditate. Play my flute. I'll be fine."

# 16

Rikli-En had spent hours pacing in his quarters, communicating with his staff and his ears throughout the Empire and its surrounding worlds, especially anxious to hear from his contacts in the Affiliated Systems and on Earth. He had supped and rested and pleased himself with two of his favorite concubines, who had done their best to distract him from the unpleasantness and ennui of life. The morning's news about the failed uprising on the plaza had been unsurprising. His father had such little imagination.

And then had come word that the final class of the Tour day was letting out. He rose from his chambers to stride down the hotel corridors of the rooms reserved for personages of the rank of Emperor, which he now occupied, to the grand meeting chamber, which was where they held the classes in this complex. His guards surrounded him in a loose, geometric pattern that provided maximum protection in closed spaces.

People streamed from the auditorium, obviously excited about what they had learned. Some came in a rush, to be greeted by officials bearing communications equipment. Rikli-En nodded to some of the slower ones, giving them a polite smile to thrill them. Then he wandered inside the room with his guards. Now that the class was over, there was no need to stop him at the door. He saw Hammon and Hammon saw him, moving quickly to bow at his side, joining his fellows in a ring around Rikli-En.

"It is possible?" Rikli-En asked quietly.

"It is indeed," Hammon said. "Anyone can do it, even me."

"You will demonstrate to me and others upon demand."

"Yes, Imperial Highness."

"And this woman? This StarFleet?" That's what his Terran operatives had called her. That and "Speaker" or somesuch.

"She is married to him, yes."

Rikli-En's eyes narrowed to cracks at that. Valiant! Married! Married to someone who could do this!

"Her name?"

"Lina Starhart," Hammon said quickly, noting his master's displeasure.

"Which one?" Rikli-En nodded at the stage where a large group of people still congregated. He'd heard that there were others with her who guided the students to make sure they were getting the technique correct. They were all quite humanoid, many with peach to cocoa complexions, which might indicate a common planet of ancestry, and might not.

The ones who did not fit the group's major skin coloring he categorized as being masters of Tishan. Thus, he dismissed the possibility of any of them being her. Tishan had not been able to do anything about Mind Control until now.

Until now.

The thought tasted sour in his mouth.

All seemed tired. Likely they were operating on stimulants; they certainly looked like they were all coming down from them. Certainly if they were working extraordinarily long days, they would have to be surviving on the stims.

"That one, Imperial Highness," the guard pointed, but Rikli-En's gaze had been diverted by one of the people in the area, a striking petite woman dressed in cream and green who was talking with several people, listening to them. Obviously not the leader of the group; she was nodding and taking advice. She tried to rub her eyes unobtrusively. It was clear that she was fighting the cessation of the stims, but she still put her effort into understanding one of the Tishana, who was lecturing or instructing her.

A student, then. Perhaps a telepath. She smiled at the Tishana, and the warmth of that smile touched Rikli-En even where he was. By the egg, she was loveliness personified. Though short in height compared to the people of the AffSys, her figure was lush. She moved, and Rikli-En's eyes drank all of her in, savoring her.

But the guard had pointed out this Lina Starhart, wife of Valiant. There she was, just beyond the lovely one's shoulder. A pretty brown-haired woman sitting in a chair. Valiant himself hovered over his new wife with concern. She had fainted or almost done so, and he was urging her now to sit up from where she'd been doubled over. She smiled at him hesitantly. He picked her up in his arms and flew out of the room.

Rikli-En studied what he could of her as she left. She was exhausted, that was plain, so tired that she'd collapsed. So she was at a weak point. She was vulnerable now at least. Who could tell if she'd be vulnerable at some later time? What kind of woman and powers could handle Valiant sexually?

"Find out where Valiant's taking her," Rikli-En said quietly to another of his guards. He looked around at the others of his five guards. "I wish to detain that one," he said. "In my ship. I shall personally check in within two hours. All of you go." One of the guards almost protested, but he gave him a steely eye. "I am safe enough here, with all these heroes and telepaths and security. Go now."

"Yes, Imperial Highness," the reluctant Hammon, the one who'd attended the meeting, said. He scuttled off with the others.

Rikli-En watched them disappear. They wouldn't be able to handle Valiant, but they could arrange a distraction or wait until he left on his own before moving in.

In the meantime there was this lovely woman. He glided up to her and caught her eye.

"If I may..." he said politely, and the others, recognizing him, moved away.

"May I help you?" she asked, and her voice was melodic, her manner well poised. She spoke Lingua without a translator. He hadn't expected that from a mere Terran.

"You may," he said. "That young woman whom Valiant just took with him..."

"That was Dinah. Dinah Stewart."

Rikli-En pushed the little surge of impatience back down. Stupid guard! He'd gotten the name wrong. Not Lina Starhart, but Dinah Stewart. "I hope she will be all right," he said, feigning interest in Valiant's wife's welfare.

"She will," the woman answered with a sigh. "She's been working hard and taking too many stims. We all just need a little rest."

"And some nourishment, perhaps," Rikli-En said kindly. "Are you cared for? You and whoever you have come with? I can furnish you with food and quiet rooms..."

"Thank you," Lina said, "but we have access to those already." She yawned in spite of herself, hiding it behind a hand. "In fact, I think it's time for me to head off to my room."

"Surely you need to eat before you sleep," Rikli-En said kindly.

"That would be the smart thing. I'll see what I can do. Thank you, Mr...?"

"Just call me Rikli-En," he said solicitously. She did not recognize him. No need to overwhelm her with his glory. "And I can call you...?"

"Carolina–"

"Where do you want us to go now?" one of her teammates interrupted, glancing at Rikli-En curiously but not recognizing him, either. Rikli-En made the guess that they were all from Earth, where the populace would not be expected to be knowledgeable about galactic current events.

"To dinner, I suppose. I think Londo should be coming back in a few minutes," Lina said in another language, the translator working for Rikli-En. So, all of the Terrans were on a first-name basis with Valiant. "They've opened up another café for us. He's got the maps for the hotel, but you can probably just ask puter. Maybe Jae has some information, or the organizers at the door."

The man nodded and moved toward the doorway of the chamber.

"Carolina," Rikli-En purred. "Perhaps you would do me the great favor of dining with me? It would be a quick meal; I realize that you need your sleep. But I would be honored..."

"Thank you so much," Lina said, "but to tell you the absolute truth, I'd rather sleep than eat. We've been on the go for – I'm not sure – a lot of days now. Really long days. Just one more to go; I know that much. Everyone wants this started now, no waiting, and I can't say that I can blame them. I've seen how many people are under control Out Here."

Out Here. She was indeed from Earth, the isolated planet. How fascinating. "Then perhaps when you awaken, you will dine with me. Bring some of your friends if you wish. It is not often that we see Terrans out this way. And it is not often that we see women of such loveliness as you."

"Thank you," she told him, "but I think I'd like to spend any extra time I can get with my husband. I–" Her eyes seemed to glaze over for a second, and she looked up as a penetrating sound shrieked through the mild uproar of the room. "What do you know?" she asked no one in particular. "He's learned to whistle."

Rikli-En turned his head to see Neutrino at the main door to the chamber, motioning to Carolina. She nodded at him. Rikli-En turned quickly away so Neutrino would not recognize him.

"Please excuse me," she said, and walked away.


Londo walked in, floating inches above the carpeting so he wouldn't disturb his sleeping wife. He didn't have to turn on any lights. He could see as if it were daylight. He went into the master bath and shut the door.

There once again he checked his sensors. His phone rang with Hal's signal and he blessed the fact that its sound wouldn't travel to the next room.

"How's it going?" Hal asked without preamble.

Lon adjusted the sensors' settings. "As well as can be expected," he replied. "Andri cut me off from call-in reports a couple hours ago. She told me to hit the sack, but there was just this one to finish. It was messy. Damn."

"What?"

"Oh, we ran into a chemical bomb at the spaceport. You know, gas as well as particulate."

"They getting desperate, are they, son?"

"It wasn't difficult to corral the perps. The hard part was getting the poison neutralized. Jae was on the other side of the city, so I used Odom and Mei."

On the screen, Hal considered. "Good choices. You had to finish cleanup?"

"*Oui.* There was a bit left after they cleared out. I set up showers for everyone nearby." Lon riffled his hair and read the new readings sourly. "Guess I wasn't as thorough as I should have been on myself. A regular shower should handle things."

"How's Lina?"

"Asleep. You know they're going three rounds now, trying to fit as many people in as they can. Three times seven hours, plus an hour, two hours of business between sessions, plus meals, and not much downtime otherwise. Per day. Mart's screaming about them being on stims too long, but he's doing what he can."

"Hm. Remember: they're only human, most of them."

"I'm mostly concerned with taking care of Lina. Everyone voted on the new schedule. No one turned it down. Mart's keeping a close eye on things. One of Lina's friends had an episode tonight, though. Mart's making sure she'll be good to go tomorrow. If not, we'll just carry on without her until she can rejoin us. I can probably get Chim to substitute if needed."

"They all know it's important, though I doubt the Terrans in the group realize just how much. Someone should throw them a parade when it's all over."

Lon laughed through his nose. "Over? Tell me again: there's going to be a time when this is over."

Hal chuckled. "Yes. Then you'll start making grandkids for me. Lots and lots of grandkids."

Londo groaned. "Are you going to say this every time I talk with you?"

"Absolutely."

Again with the snort. "We have to get Aldierra through their Doomsday Deadline," he reminded his father.

"Then after that. You should be settled in by then. Will Starhaven be finished? Lina needs a permanent home to build a family. At least that's the impression I had of her when I spoke with her. At heart she's an old-fashioned girl, a norm though she isn't, Lon, in a brand-new, upside-down, non-norm world. It's up to you to see to the things she needs for stability. Emotional support. That… family of hers… Well, you – and I – are her new family now. Mom and Dad will help out too."

Lon smiled at his father. "It'll be good for her. For me as well."

"For all of us," Hal assured him.

Lina awakened when the bed shifted. Someone was climbing in.

Granger! Paul Granger, the rogue Galactic Guard! Danger! Disaster! He was after her, trying to kill her, rape her! Torture her!

Lina rose up with a lurch, a scream on her lips as a man's hand closed around her upper arm.

"*Chérie*, it's me, it's me!"

Londo.

Londo!

She threw her arms around him and burst into tears. He rocked her as she cried.

"Tell me about it. Tell me everything."

She shook her head against his chest and he sighed. "Okay, kitten. That's okay. You've been on stims and all this general craziness. You'll tell me when you're ready? Or you'll tell Jae?"

Lina nodded under his chin and hung on for safety.

"One more day. I can do it," she assured him as she shook.

"Shh. Shh. You're safe. You're safe here with me."

She never knew when she fell asleep.

There were no translators on board his docked ship and so Rikli-En could not understand the babblings of Valiant's pathetic bride as she most likely begged for mercy, begged for her life. He did feel some pity for her; he could see how Valiant might like her liquid brown eyes, her long fingers. A nicely turned body, quite inviting. He took care to take things slowly, to draw things out and not rush the experience. He wanted his tape of the procedures to be quite thorough.

But where usually he'd take care of the first rape personally, now he found he was not in the mood for sexual torture, so he instructed his guards and some of the more specialized personnel on his ship to take over for him as he watched, overlooking the recording process. How far should he go with this? It was a delicate matter and he considered, tapping his fingers against his chin as he watched.

His father the emperor would want his own copy, of course. And one for Valiant, probably one for Maximus as well. He made sure he was not in any of the recording, that only his employees and slaves were. If they made reference to anyone, it was to the emperor and not to him. After all, he respected the power that Valiant and Maximus personified. It would not do to have both of them on a blood trail to him.

Instead of waiting how many more decades, maybe even a century, this situation might bump up the day of his succession by a significant degree. Rikli could be emperor within a month if he played this right.

The woman Dinah finally sank into complete unconsciousness. Even the pain of her torture couldn't rouse her. Blood loss would have weakened her as well. Perhaps they shouldn't have spilled quite so much. It would do no good to try to wake her at this point. She had reached the limit of stims. Her mind would be senseless, no good for a full torture. Sooner or later she'd awaken naturally. Then if she tried to retreat into unconsciousness again, they would do something about it.

He dismissed everyone for the night and decided to get some rest himself.

# 17

Dawn broke gently on this world, and Rikli-En regretted that it was no longer possible to consider this planet a future member of the Empire, at least not for a few years at the very least. Ah well. These things happened. After he ascended the throne, he'd certainly build toward the option of invasion. He consulted the Tour's schedule and waited a few hours, getting some mundane business finished before he strolled down a hotel hallway, his bodyguards within calling distance but instructed to stay out of visual range of him. There was a guard up ahead. Not a Legionnaire.

"Some of the Terran delegation is housed in this corridor, is it not?" He smiled as he questioned the guard.

"Sir..."

"Imperial Highness," he corrected.

"H-highness," the guard stuttered. "Yes, it is. But I'm afraid that absolute security measures are in effect now. There's been an incident. A Legionnaire has been killed. Or wounded; I'm not sure. There's a 'Do Not Disturb' notice on this suite that's red-labelled. You cannot advance any farther. We are on short staff at the moment."

"But I am a guest of the woman named Carolina," Rikli-En said gently. Was that her entire name? Was it Caro Lina? She'd said it all together.

"I'm sorry," the guard said and glanced to a padd floating at his side. "I don't have you on a list..."

"Of course not, you fool." Rikli-En let the sound of absolute, ruling power enter his voice. "She has only just summoned me, now that she is awake. She would like me to breakfast with her."

"I..." the guard hesitated. This was Rikli-En.

"I commend your efforts," Rikli-En purred. "I wish my own guards were as stringent in their caution. But I can assure you that I am expected. You may scan me if you wish. I am not a common... assassin."

"Of course not, sir," the guard was now deferential. "I suppose... since it is you..." He snapped to attention and led Rikli-En down the hallway, stopping at a door. "Your Highness. Imperial Highness," he finally said, and bowed.

"That will be all." Rikli-En didn't look at him as he stepped through the doorway.

What lay beyond was one of those lush, jungly green rooms the people here liked so much, with faux-glass ceilings and tiled floors and furniture scattered around thick plantings of leafy, blooming trees. He could see the purpled sky of dawn outside on the room's screens, and there were various birds here, or singing insects, that were waking up with the faux day.

He knew that another class began in a little over an hour. Over there was movement, just beyond that stand of potted bushes. It stopped as he approached. He made his thoughts benign, friendly, the kind of thoughts that would not alarm a telepath like these Terrans must be.

She was gowned in white satin that flowed down to the floor. She had been brushing her hair, unbound now, long and auburn, curling far down her back. How pleasant, that she was only a few inches shorter than he.

"What are you doing here?" she asked roughly. "Who let you in?"

"I merely told the guard that you had invited me to breakfast," Rikli-En said as he sat next to a food cart. "It was a little presumptuous of me, but every now and then I enjoy being presumptuous." He leaned back to look at her, to watch the way the material of her gown clung to her as she set her brush down, watching him warily. An odd red glow came from beneath her bodice. "There's nothing to be afraid of. I'm really quite harmless, I assure you. Just consider me... I know. An admirer. An admirer of beauty."

"Don't even try to get any closer to her," a male voice said, a voice tipped with steel and worse. A very familiar voice: Valiant's.

Rikli-En flinched and tried not to look like he had.


"What's he been up to?" Londo asked Lina. He wasn't wearing his vest, but otherwise was in full costume.

Relief flooded her now that Lon was here. "He just now came in. He said the guard had let him in when he told him that I'd invited him to breakfast."

"Invited him?" Lon gave a harsh laugh. "That's one guard who is out of a job. Where'd you get that idea, Rikli-En? Don't they serve breakfast in the Imperial Suites?"

"Imperial?" Lina was puzzled. "Who is this guy, anyway? He came up to me after the class last night."

"And you invited him to breakfast?" Londo asked.

Lina smiled tightly. "Hardly. I said I wished to spend any spare time with my husband. I repeat, who's the creep?"

"Introduce yourself, Rikli-En." Lon took another step closer to him. A dangerous step; Rikli-En should know his life depended on how he acted.

"I am always eager to introduce myself to charming and beautiful women," he said. "I am Rikli-En, Prince of the Inner Ring of Five Planets, Duke of the High Houses of Weshor–"

"Etcetera, etcetera," Lon said harshly. "Heir apparent – or apparent in his own mind – to the imperial throne of Yanist-Glory. Glory-boy's oldest semi-legitimate son."

Lina hissed, drawing back.

"Rikli-En," Londo drawled in a formal introduction, "may I introduce my wife, Carolina Starhart."

*Wife? This one?*

"What?!" Lina gasped as the intruder's startled thoughts broadcast. She moved forward, but Londo set himself between the two of them. "What have you done?"

"With whom?" Londo said, keeping himself between the two of them. **There's no telling what Rikli-En has up his perverted sleeve.**

**He's confused. He's done something with someone...** "It's Dinah!" Lina exclaimed. "He thought she was me. It... He's *torturing* her!"

Londo reached to grab Rikli-En by the collar, forcing his face inches away from his own. Shaking him. "Where is she, Rik? Tell us! Tell us!"

"I don't have any–"

"Got it." Lina's voice was dark with anger. She could see the location in Rikli-En's mind to port to.

"Okay. Quick in, quick out, catch them unaware. I take care of any guards, you take care of her. Jae!"

Lina nodded and heard the echoed response from Jae. Something else was happening... "Got it. And him?"

Lon kept his fist on Rikli-en's collar. "He goes with us, too. He'll make a good shield in case they have energy weapons. Ready?"

"Ready."

"Go."

They appeared in a dimly lit ship's cabin, a narrow bed/couch along one wall, toilet facilities along another, open to view by a guard. Recording equipment was stored in piles or floating lazily in the air. A half-dozen weapons lay within the guard's reach, although Lon knew that Lina wouldn't recognize any of them. She didn't have to.

Rikli-En gasped at the sudden change of scenery. "She has non-psi powers," he noted in a blithe tone. "I'd heard a rumor. Impressive. What have we here?"

A deathly pale Dinah sprawled naked on the bed. Dark puddles of blood dripped from it onto the floor. She moaned and twitched even as she lay senseless. She had bruises all over. Cuts. Gashes. Skin peeled back. Implements sticking out from her belly, from her neck and breasts and face.

"Her eye…" Lina gasped.

The guard jerked at the sudden appearance and Lon held Rikli-En in the air between them. "Make a move," he growled, keeping the body of the heir as a shield. He stomped quickly, deliberately into the guard's area. "Give me a reason to do something to him," he warned, and the guard stayed frozen where he was. Lon searched for the recording crystal. There. He punched a button and a slot spat it out. No copies had yet been made.

It only took a finger tap on the guard's forehead to knock him out. Lon gave an order to his Legion ring and then grabbed the crystal before checking Lina. She cradled Dinah in her arms; the woman was still unconscious. She looked anxiously at Londo and he nodded.

They were back in the garden room.

"Medical facilities," Lina croaked. "Where?"

They ported again, to Londo's vision of a hospital. Lina, her white gown now soaked with blood, gently levitated Dinah with all the skill she could muster. She ported in a sheet from their bedroom to wrap her with. Doctors and nurses rushed to their aid, and as Lina went off with them to answer as many questions as she could, Londo trailed behind. He kept himself and Rikli behind privacy curtain screens. Lina positioned herself so she could answer questions from the doctors and still hear Londo's conversation.

"Your diplomatic immunity isn't going to save you this time, Rikli," Londo snapped as he shook him. "We've got you. We're going to put you out of action for good."

"Ouch. I don't know what you're talking about, Londo." Rikli-En tried to sound hurt. "Do you think that I'm on that crystal? Torturing or raping that poor woman? I assure you, I had nothing to do with this. Nothing at all."

Lina's fury and fear and guilt radiated through the curtains separating them.

"Telepathic evidence has never been admissible," Rikli reminded Londo. "If some of my... employees are criminals, why believe me, I will happily and most willingly turn them over to the local authorities. Anyone who would do something like this belongs in the deepest dungeon they have around here! Such depravity." Rikli-En's face held the faintest ghost of a smile. "Such good luck that whoever was responsible for this didn't get their hands on your lovely wife, Londo. I shudder to think what might have happened."

Lon's eyes involuntarily glanced beyond the curtains at Lina for an instant. The robe she'd since ported on didn't entirely cover all the blood on her.

"I'll make a full report myself of this matter to the emperor," Rikli-En said. "I'm sure he'll want to know *all* the details."

Lina stepped around the curtains for a moment. "Let me port him between worlds, Londo," she snarled. "I can drop him into nothingness. Let him remain *outside* the universe for five minutes so he dissolves. There won't be a molecule left to autopsy."

The Heir's eyes opened wide.

For three long seconds Lon seriously considered giving his permission. Instead he told Rikli, "I have already informed the emperor what he might expect if anything were ever to happen to Lina and be remotely traceable to him. I'll expand that now to include tracing back to any of his kin. You tell him that. Tell him to keep you in line."

The medical staff feverishly worked on Dinah. Lina tried to work on her auric field to help healing, but was too upset to do much. Instead she returned to Londo's side of the curtain to stand defiantly in front of Rikli-En, her eyes glinting of justice to be served. From within her robe came that glow again, now brighter... as if it were angry.

"I know you now," she said, and her voice was danger itself. "I know you and your vibrations. I know how those who work for you feel. You had a hireling at the class yesterday. I see that now. I'll be on guard for you. I've set spirit watches to warn of your presence. There is no way for you to get near me again." Londo knew that this was not only for Rikli-En's benefit but to calm himself, as well. "So don't even try."

"A worthy consort," Rikli-En finally said.

"With many powerful friends," Londo warned, "who would be eager for vengeance if anything ever happened. Not that there'd be much left of whoever it was who had ordered it in the first place."

"I have always found that it is the challenges in life that keep it interesting."

The doctors stabilized and then secured Dinah in a stasis cocoon where time and pain could not touch her.

Lina sought Lon's comforting arms once again. "I thought it was just my PTSD bothering me this past day," she moaned. "I was trying to smash it down until we get to a point… a point where I can see someone."

"Yes, yes."

"No wonder I was having such nightmares. I must have been seeing a little of what was happening to her. The stims…"

"Yes. Yes."

Ruefully she backed up from him. They had things to do. She rubbed her tears out of his shirt. "I'm going to get some waterproofing spray for your clothes. And Jae's. Ah, god. If only…"

"Woulda, coulda, shoulda."

She nodded.


Through that veil of shock, Lina heard Londo hold a muttered conversation through his Legion ring, and within minutes they'd all four, Londo, Lina, Rikli, and Dinah's cocoon, ported into the Legion's makeshift command center on the planet.

There were two other cocoons sitting on the floor between long tables containing active electronic maps and charts. "Who–" Lina began even as Londo scanned them with his paravision. His was quicker than her clairvoyance, but she could see through his eyes.

Erik. The carefree young Legionnaire who had worked so hard to get on Jae's Alpha Team and befriended Lina during her imprisonment. And Dr. Mart.

Jae and Dr. Benton crouched next to Erik's cocoon, checking its readouts. That large insect Legionnaire knelt behind Jae in conference. All looked up in shock at the newcomers.

Stoan was there along with a handful of other Legionnaires. "Is she all right?" he blurted when he saw Lina's bloody condition.

"The blood's not hers," Londo said.

Stoan eyed the new cocoon. "Stewart?" he asked.

Before Lina could say anything, Lon reported, "She was tortured. Badly injured."

Stoan nodded. "We'll take care of her back at HQ, for as long as needed."

Lina breathed a sigh of as much relief as she could gather to herself. At Mega-Legion Headquarters on Sarastor, Dinah would be treated like an honored Legionnaire. She knew the Legion had the absolute best medical staff and wondrous equipment. They had to, being the powerful army they were and facing the dangers they did. That's where Demi was being stored as well. Riz and her staff would take good care of her friends.

"How—"

"Mart was responding to the medical emergency last night."

Around all the blood memories flooding through her mind, Lina tried to remember. Last night was so far off. That's right; Dinah had fainted after the last session. Lon had taken her to her room and called for the doctor to double-check that she would be okay. Lon had been called out on a mission right after that.

Lina had assumed that Dinah would be fine. Dr. Mart would yell at them for using so many stims, but…

Erik had been guarding Dinah's door. The doctor had signaled from the end of the corridor for admittance, Erik had gone to do that…

And ten terrorists firing weapons had descended out of nowhere.

Close quarters. Erik had managed a distress call even as he dragged the wounded Mart out of the way, but the hotel was a warren of old-fashioned hallways and planetary guards who weren't linked completely into the Legion's systems. It took time for help to reach Erik. Between the attackers' weaponry and Erik's control of wind and atmospheric temperature – not the best choice of powers for an interior battle – the corridor and rooms around it had been left in ruins. Four of the attackers were killed. Two more were easily tracked by their blood trails. The others had vanished.

Dr. Mart had barely survived, but was missing his left forearm in addition to other grave injuries. Erik's Legion battle armor hadn't fully deployed in time. His arms, legs and feet had been hard-pierced with weapons fire.

Legion forces conducted immediate checks of the Tour participants roomed in neighboring areas. Only one person was missing.

"Rikli thought she was Lina." Londo held the heir in the air by his collar. In his other hand he brandished the recording crystal.

The Legion commander regarded Rikli without a shred of emotion showing on his face. "Rikli-En," he said and turned to his second-in-command, Andri.

"Diplomatic problems," she noted around clenched teeth. "Likely it will take weeks to figure out what needs to be done with him. Legally."

Stoan turned back. "I'd hate to see him harmed while the politicos decide his fate," he told no one in particular. "In the meantime we'll keep him in safekeeping. Londo?"

Lon eyed his prisoner. "I'm thinking the force field section. Just in case. I don't think there are any electronic signals that can penetrate it. Very solitary confinement."

Stoan glanced at Andri for her opinion before including Lina in his nod. "The quick way then. I don't want to look at his face on our way home. I'll turn on the force fields from here."

Andri put in, "I'm not sure who would be in charge of issuing rations or seeing to temperature controls down there. I'll have to research. Maybe after we get back."

That made the side of Stoan's mouth twitch.

Lon pictured a cell deep in the Sarastoran headquarters in his mind so Lina could see it as well.

"Shall I give him the long tour there? The six-minute one?" she asked. The stims pushed her anger to overload levels, and she didn't care.

Stoan's eyebrows rose. He knew her five-minute limit for porting. He licked his lips as he considered. "The quickest way, please, Speaker," he decided. "Perhaps for his trip back to Daddy we can send him the long way."

With a nod, Lina ported Rikli-En to prison.


There was nothing more at the moment to do for Dinah or Erik or Mart. After a few comforting words to Lina, Londo flew off to make sure that Rikli-En's ship would be left undisturbed as evidence. Lon and Jae both guaranteed her that Rikli would pay dearly, despite his position. Even before the AffSys legal system could punish him, likely Rikli's father would do a more thorough job for getting caught.

Back in their room, Lina cleaned herself up and took many calming breaths that didn't work well.

*I will brazen through this,* she ordered herself. *I will tough it out. Just for a day. Tomorrow I'll see one of those shrinks. Tomorrow's not that far away. I can do this.*

She ported to the hotel's conference auditorium. There were many more Legion guards than normal, and she'd made sure they knew she was about to arrive. There she calmly explained to the waiting crowd that the day's classes would be delayed by at least two hours, maybe three. The classes would also last a little longer, since the teaching staff was down by one – but the number of classes would still stand.

That staff reeled in shock at the news Lina gave them. Of course all the Terrans had been good friends with Dinah. Lina assured them that she'd receive miraculous physical and mental care. "Same as Olympia," she said. They'd all seen the startling press conference about Demi's near-fatal battle.

They discussed how best to face the classes as Lina felt herself fading farther and farther from them, as if they were down a long, dark corridor. Their voices echoed around her.

Her people would be trying to do intricate psychic work while under emotional strain.

"Should we put off the classes a day?" Lina managed to ask them. She knew the distance was all an illusion, but still forced herself not to shout so they could hear her from where they were.

She needed a stim. She needed some of those drugs Jae took to calm himself. Who was that substitute doctor? The one from Lon's team? She couldn't recall. Everything was… Everything was…

Blood in that hallway. Laser fire and fog. Explosions ripping up the beach, leaving Londo lying dead. The freezing wind howling over the blast of too-close jet engines as she fell from that plane. Granger bending over her, laughing in horrible triumph. Stoan exhorting the Legion to lobotomize her. Dinah: a blood-oozing pit where her eye should have been.

That bully in sixth grade beating her up, sending her to the hospital. Dad leaving her to rot on the cold basement floor when she was eight, blood dripping from her leg. Having to make a decision whether she wanted to die or live, disconnected from the rest of humanity.

Blood, blood, blood!

"Tomorrow will be as bad as today." David decided for the group. "Only by then we'll have had time to worry about our own safety. It might be worse."

One of the Tishana, Buntic, said, "If we focus, we can get through this."

Lina could do the same. But there was blood and gore and mud and burning flesh up to her hips. She tried to wade through it, but it was so far…

She didn't want to move. She was stuck. Better that than put herself and her friends at risk again.

A doctor. Please, a doctor… Lon. Jae. Get a doctor…

The others agreed that free time wouldn't accomplish much.

This was duty. This was helping people. She'd promised. She'd vowed. "The… the second anyone starts feeling like they can't… The second…"

At the end of that infinite tunnel, she could feel the presence of someone new. She tried to see through the red fog and laser fire, but had to duck from it. Hide. Stay safe! Nowhere was safe. Everywhere was pure, solidified terror. It sucked at her very soul. Where could she go? What could she do?

She was alone.

Everything was trying to kill her!

"By the orb!" she heard the new voice say.

# 18

"Here we go, here we go," Jae's gentle voice reassured her. "We're here, kitten. Relax." "You're safe."

Lina tried to take a breath and didn't quite make it. The second try summoned enough oxygen to allow her to try another time.

"Better?" Daisley asked.

"Oh." Lina breathed deeply. Breathe in safety. Breathe out fear. Jae and Lon were here. Breathe. Breathe.

"I think I'll have that breakdown now," she managed to whisper.

The lasers again! The booming down the corridors! The roar of the cannons that had brought Londo down! Her fractured leg! The groans from Dinah! The cries from Demi! She was on the cot in Legion HQ, unable to breathe. Dying.

Here were Jae and Lon. Safe? Yes, they were.

She could feel them so steady, and when she opened her eyes they were there, squatting next to where she lay on some divan or cot. There too was Daisley, and behind her, Andri and Chimrin. They were in a new room, by themselves. Andri was studying her, but Chim had her arms crossed in front of herself, scowling.

Jae and Londo's faces were full of concern. Wonderful Jae and Londo.

"Thank God for you two," she told them, though she wasn't sure if the words actually escaped her mouth. Still, they smiled at her. Patted her arm and rubbed her knuckles.

Love, love, love. She tried to make that her primary emotion. Push the fear away. Push the danger back.

A mask covered her nose and mouth. Oh. She breathed full breaths, concentrating on exchanging good energy for the bad along with the oxygen she was likely getting.

"Fully conscious?" Andri asked Daisley.

"Yes, Subcommander. Well, pretty much."

"Good. Don't do that again, Lina. We have your people with counselors. The classes are being postponed as long as this round takes. We have a counselor waiting for you as well."

"She needs about six," Chimrin muttered. "Idiot. You should have asked for help long before this. Look at what holding out cost you."

"Chim!" Lon and Jae exclaimed as one.

"I'm not going to coddle her like you two. When both of you came to the Legion, I didn't say, 'Let's wait until they have time. Until they're desperate for help.' No, I shuttled each of you off to intensive psychiatric work first thing."

"Sorry," Lina said.

"It's okay to ask for help," Jae told her.

But she'd always had to do things herself. All her life.

"We're here now," he reminded her.

Wonderful Jae. Wonderful Londo.

She held them both back. Why couldn't she be strong? Tears rolled down her cheeks. So ashamed. Why did she do this? Why couldn't she handle this? Oh Jesus, Dinah! She'd betrayed her friend. Shouldn't have let her come along. Stupid Muttbutt! Stupid, stupid!

"Kitten." Londo gathered her to his chest.

The door opened for Dr. Benton, who briskly took stock of things before waving Daisley aside. "I did the research," she told her colleague. "Not much info on this many stims, but I think my dosages are correct. Three more classes, is that right?"

Lina buried her head in Lon's chest even as she reached so Jae could squeeze her hand.

Then there was a slight sting at her neck.

She blinked. Stopped breathing for a moment, but then it was easier to breathe. Easier to think.

Dr. Benton glared at her. "You will take two – let me repeat, two – full rest days after this Tour. No more stims of any type for at least four weeks. Let's make that six. This includes that caffeinated drink you like."

"No tea," Lina confirmed even as Londo echoed that, but in the form of an order.

"And you will begin psychiatric counseling immediately."

Lina took a breath. "Yes," she said.

"Yes," Jae and Londo reinforced in unison.

She felt like someone had wrung her out like a dishrag. In a while she had a class to supervise. "I'm going to need–"

"I will personally supervise stims for the rest of the Tour," Benton intoned. "For you and the other staffers. This has gone on far too long. Mart should have–"

"Mart tried to talk us out of it," Lina said miserably. "Don't blame Mart. We insisted."

Poor Mart! Mart would be okay. He *must* be okay. And Erik. And Dinah. And Demi. Legion Medical would cure them all, bring them back even better than before.

The Great and Powerful Wizard would grant their wishes.

"I'm not doing too well here," she murmured.

"Better than you were," Lon said.

She nodded. "It's gonna come back, isn't it? It is. This is just temporary sanity. Gotta lead class. Don't want to break down again in front of everyone."

"In a while," Jae said. "Let's have you meet a counselor first. Just say hello, establish ground rules. You can do that much."

"Just a few minutes," Lina said. They had a sector to save. "I'll need a doctor standing by during classes. For me. For anyone else too.

"But first," she decided, "I want to speak to my husbands. Alone."


Lon closed the door behind the others, ensuring privacy.

Just in time. Lina dissolved into loud sobs.

"Sorry. I'm so sorry!"

Jae took her in his arms and let her cry on his shoulder, rubbing her back as he kissed the top of her head.

"How... How many more people are going to be hurt?" she managed to ask. "How many more? Oh god, oh god."

"How many more people are going to be helped?" he asked her gently. "How many worlds are safe from Yanist-Glory now? How many lives are going to be freed from Mind Control, free from even worrying about it?"

She shook her head against him. No time for logic now, just get rid of the fear, the anguish, the guilt.

Lon sat on the cot next to them. He rubbed both their backs.

"Tell us now," he urged quietly. "Tell us everything you want to get out."

"Yes. Yes, now. Oh god, oh god, I was so scared." She whimpered. "With Granger. I was all alone and it was dark and they had that damned shackle on me and I couldn't do anything and I was so, so scared. I knew I was going to die. I didn't want to die without seeing you again. Both of you. I wrote notes to you. Ah god, I'm such a coward..."

She told them everything she could think of, which was leaving out a lot that they'd get to eventually. She told them of her life as a norm where nothing like any of this ever, *ever* happened, and then it all hit, like someone had fired a gun to signal disaster.

Anguish from Lon.

"Not you, not you," she tried to assure him. "I had an idea what I was getting into by then."

He tried to *argue* with her.

"Shut up. What is, is. I'm not letting you go. Or you either, Jae, so don't even think about it. Not that easy. I claim you. Both. Individually and as a couple.

"I'll get used to this. No, I won't. But I'll get counseling. Right now. I promise. Every week, like you said."

She hiccupped. "Doctor's orders. I'll follow them. Gotta get things done. Gotta get—"

"That means taking care of yourself first."

Breathe. Breathe.

They spoke gentle encouragements to her. They told her how much they loved her.

That was wondrous. They cuddled her in their love and caring and kissed her head from both sides. Lina could feel weight lifting from her shoulders. From the bridge of her nose as well. And the top of her cheeks. The body held tension in odd places.

She breathed out even more existential weight. Breathed it out again. Then she took a clean, full breath.

"God, I miss my cats," she managed before she straightened up. She blinked twice.

Lon handed her a nutridrink. Dutifully she took a sip. It didn't taste like much. Needed cherry flavoring or maybe lemon-lime. Maybe she was too depressed to taste anything. "Oh god, I don't have to repeat all that for my journal, do I?"

"We'll just copy it," Jae said. "I'll see to it."

"Oh, good. Are we good? For now?"

Lon and Jae looked at each other to exchange silent thoughts before turning back to her.

"For now," Londo said. He handed a drink to Jae as well. Lina suspected that one had alcohol in it.

"To be continued."

"As needed," Lon added, and Jae nodded. "I've been thinking. This is what married people do: handle things together. It'll be easier than just doing it yourself. Kitten, sometimes things come up that you just can't handle alone."

"Do you really have problems like this?" Lina asked.

"Unfortunately all the time." Lon took a sip of his own drink. "When I feel I'm getting overwhelmed I go to my therapist or Hal or my friends or teammates."

Lina's gaze shifted to Jae.

"Same here. I have more therapists than Londo, though. Mine are better than his."

Lon gave a snort. Then he turned deadly serious. "I want you to come with me next time I see Adam," he told Jae. "I've got to… I want you there to…"

"I said I forgave you."

Londo ran both palms down his face, dragging his features downward. "It was unforgiveable, what I did."

"Nothing's unforgiveable," Lina put in. "What's going on?"

Lon licked his lips before saying, "I told Jae I didn't want him anymore. After I'd made up my mind to marry you."

Lina caught her breath. That was what the Three Worlds had tried to show her at the Initiation. She'd been too busy seeing that Londo was in love with someone else to consider the full import.

"That's not what you said. You said you couldn't see me anymore. Not in that way," Jae said.

"I turned you away. You!" Now Lon's hands covered his eyes as his entire body slumped. "I… rejected you. How could I have done that? What was I thinking?"

Jae looked to Lina. "He did say he was open to asking you about a threeway."

"After. After I told you to go away!"

Lon's energy curled up. This was what people called being "tied in knots." Could she help? She asked her guardian angel to ask his.

Jae wrapped himself around Lon's back, his chin on Lon's head. "I forgive you. I forgive you."

"Londo," Lina said hesitantly. "If I can say something. As a loving wife. People kept telling me you were a liar. That you lied to make your life easier or for things to go faster."

Londo shook his head, never looking up. "I will never lie to you again."

"That's fine and I really appreciate the promise. But… this was just after you'd recovered, right? When you'd only found out a day or two before that you could have sex with someone? That you could touch me without killing me?"

He nodded as Jae stroked his hair.

"Your emotions were in a complete flux. You were off-balance. You were upside-down." Lina tried to word it right. "Could it be… you lied to yourself?"

Jae looked up at her.

"You could no more give up Jae than you could give up breathing," Lina told him as well as Lon. "You've been lovers – not physically, but emotionally – for ages. There was no way you could quit the other. You lied, Londo. To yourself."

"Stop beating yourself up, Lon love," Jae whispered. "You scared me. Yes, you broke my heart. But it didn't last long. Within, oh, five minutes we were talking the possibility of an open marriage. I knew we could make it work."

"Maybe not an open marriage," Lina said, "but a Triune. Once Jae explained it to me – and he used charts, Lon, *charts*– I had to agree it was the only way to go. You two were together long before I arrived."

"How could I have betrayed you, Jae, even for five minutes?"

"You tried to ditch me too, Londo," Lina reminded him. "Back when your powers returned on the island. You lie to yourself. You hurt yourself when you do so, as well as those around you. You have to stop doing that."

"Yes, Londo," Jae said. He hugged Lon around the neck. "I don't want to see you hurt."

Lon's heavy sigh carried a lot of negative energy with it. He closed his eyes and touched Jae's arm. "I'm sorry. I'm so sorry."

"We'll tell Adam about it together. And Saichan as well. Maybe we'll throw a therapy party; everyone including Lina? Get it all out?"

"I'm sorry, Jae," Lina said. "I had my own ideas about what your manic condition was. I know it all, right? And I diagnosed you. Played it down. I was wrong."

His head tilted as he listened.

"You know how best to treat yourself. You're dealing with your own demons. You have doctors and therapists to help you. I promise to listen to what you and they advise, and to help as I can. As you let me. I won't assume I'm omniscient."

Jae scratched the back of his neck, looking thoughtful. "Apology accepted. I knew you were coming from a caring direction, Lie-Lie. What you said had a lot of truth to it. I had been wallowing. Poor, miserable me. Well."

He looked sharply at the two of them. "All this baring of hearts brings up another slant: we need to talk about the new relationship. In the past I may have used sex as a kind of ad hoc psychotherapy," he admitted. "Guess that's over?"

"Bite your tongue!" Lon exclaimed even as Lina barked a sound of rebuke.

Lon sat straight up and turned to be nose to nose with his husband. "You will just target your sexual urges to two specific people," he ordered.

"We need to have a talk real soon about that, too," Lina said. "We have schedules. We need to add a category, make sure it doesn't get overlooked."

"Okay. And we also make sure schedules include therapy," Jae insisted. "We muddle through but we do this together."

# 19

Three hours later the last day of sessions began. It was crazy late, but there had been assassins and kidnapping and grievous wounds. Everyone agreed that it was quite understandable. The participants were happy to have made it to this, the final classes of the Tour, so all worked out for the best.

It was terrible to know of the attack and still try to function. It was beyond difficult. But periodically throughout the long day Lina gathered her people around her and gestured toward the audience. "See them," she instructed, taking care to pay attention to her own advice for once. "Look at how we're helping them. Helping the people of their worlds. Imagine the good we're doing. We need to keep going, keep the good circulating."

The Tishana did a breathing thing to calm themselves, and Lina had them teach it to everyone. Big breaths in; big exhales. The trick was to gather free energies from a large area around themselves, not just inside them, and release the toxic ones. They imagined color changes in the energies as they did it. Lina had everyone funnel their exhales down into the core of the planet they were on, where the energies could be converted to higher vibrations.

Playing the flute frequently helped as well.

Three classes later and after dinner and a quick conference with Lon, Jae, and two Tour coordinators, Lina told everyone to sleep in. Trips home would start when they started. Everyone was to get rest, order a fancy delivered breakfast, and enjoy the perks their rooms provided. The assistants all gave a weak, if sad, cheer.

The final assassin of the group of ten had just been found, dead of a self-inflicted shot.

No more classes. Lina woke too emotionally exhausted to celebrate. Much. Her staff had been sent home via ships, not ports, with assurances that their promised interstellar tours and pay would happen as soon as could be arranged. Everyone would be kept apprised of Dinah, Mart and Erik's recoveries.

There were other things to tie up before the Starharts got their two days of rest and recovery. (And maybe they'd fudge a bit on that second day, get some work done, but at a relaxed pace.) There would be a concluding press conference, this time with all three of them present.

She'd have to look official, not New Age-y. Lina ported to Lon's – to *their* – apartment at Legion HQ on Sarastor and checked through its closet. There was the dress she'd worn to her trial… which had turned into the Three Worlds Investiture, which would become more and more publicized as time went by. It might thus have some kind of "official" status. She liked the outfit. She had designed it in hopes of attending a fantasy con, and it satisfied Legion Protocol's body-coverage requirements. But…

She ported it on. The capelet was too much. Lon had added it as an impressive frou-frou. Lina removed it, which took the attached stiff, long sleeves as well. Now it was a light summer dress with a square neckline and handkerchief hem. She'd designed the fabric as an ombre with a pattern of spring green and cream to invoke leafy shadows. The soled, sheer tights underneath were darker but also gradated to a dappled forest green.

She studied her reflection in Lon's – *their* – full-size, 3D bedroom mirror. She'd been falling a lot lately. Flying, floating, thrown to super-heated ground. Kicked out of a plane at high altitude. Hopefully most of that wouldn't be happening in the future, but you never knew.

A skirt wouldn't do if this were to be her go-to public outfit. Her *costume*. What a concept.

Instead she had the computer show her a variant where the dress was actually a fitted bodice over an open skirt that overlapped a few inches in front and was made of that same breezy fabric as before. A generous hemline, still handkerchief in style, allowed it to billow in a satisfying way. She gave it a satiny ruched belt. The tights became opaque so no one's eyebrows would raise if the skirt opened or flew up with movement. Of course those tights were standard Sarastoran soled ones, because pants and sneakers didn't come more comfy than those.

***Lon? Jae?*** she asked as her husbands prepared for the day in some Traim restaurant, though it held strong bar vibes. ***I haven't had a chance to research Feithi fashion to do anything that would conform to that, but we're all going to have* *to make adjustments in that direction sooner or later. This is pre-whatever that is going to be.***

They studied the images that their Legion rings showed them for a much longer time than Lina would have thought needed. And they discussed it verbally, not letting her hear their conversation. Finally the decision came back:

***Sleeves.*** This from the both of them, with emphasis.

Drat. But she sent them variant designs: full sleeve, three-quarter, sheer and solid. They compromised on the three-quarter in fabric that matched the rest of the dress.

***I'll slide it by Protocol,*** Jae promised her, though Lon didn't seem optimistic about its chances.

Lina ordered the final design, found it in the replicator a few minutes later, and put it on before porting back to… wherever they'd been.


She was getting used to press conferences, especially those held in the shadow of disaster. Halfway through this one, Lina felt something… shift on her chest.

No, the Ruby was still securely fastened under her clothing, but it was stirring *inwardly.*

"What is it?" Jae whispered to her.

"Granger. It still has a link to him. He's stable enough to be moved."

***Good timing at least,*** Lon told them as a reporter finished asking a lengthy question about the Legion's continued presence on Deseed, the world they'd begun on. The world that had seen a planetary war two weeks before. They let Stoan handle that. ***We'll see to him before we hit Aldierra, contact the Galactic Sentinels.***

Lina tried not to let the Ruby's anxiety affect her as the conference wound up. ***We won't let him near you,*** she assured it. ***We'll make sure the Sentinels know what you've been through, and that they treat you right. Do they have counseling for Rubies? We'll get you some somehow. And a nice vacation.*** It was such a sweet, brave Ruby.

And counseling… Counseling wasn't that frightening. You just talked. The counselor listened and replied like a normal person, though they took notes. Even if they didn't write things down, Lina could still see the flick of an eye, the crook of a finger that said a computer was supposed to add that piece to its data.

They would use the preliminary appointment to decide who and what would work best for her. In the meantime she had very mild but timed doses of something that was keeping her a little calmer than normal. And she assured everyone that she was taking time to breathe.

The press' questions went on and on. There were a thousand reporters present and all cameras, visible and invisible, were primarily focused on the three of them, with the unfortunate emphasis on *her*. When Lon or Jae would speak, Lina took her deep breaths and reminded herself that she could handle this. Four weeks ago? No way. She would have been flailing around on the rug like a fish out of water. Now… Yes. *This too shall pass*. Or at least she'd get used to it at some level.

They took turns answering the general questions, but it was up to Lina to handle the Mind Control-specific answers. These people just did not believe that Mind Control could be stopped.

Jae leaned forward. "We can do it; it's been done. When you return to your home planets, most of you, you'll find that the technique is already available to learn and utilize. If it isn't where you are, it soon will be, as in a matter of days. Everyone should–"

His attention was caught by the red glow originating around Lina's chest. It grew into a definite basketball shape, then expanded until it encased the three of them on the podium.

"We are being summoned," Lina announced.

Jae had the presence of mind to tap his Legion ring. "Dr. Mem-Bazer, please prepare to monitor the ports."

"Oh, right," Lina murmured, and Wiley's tracker bracelet appeared on her wrist.

"Subcommander Nurunori, secure our gear. We will be returning for it," Londo managed to say before Lina ported them out.


They arrived in the Washington hospital's private waiting room, the one that Lina and the Ruby had done an excellent job of accidentally half-destroying the other day as the Ruby recharged. Now its reconstruction was almost finished. The ParaNet must have aided the repairs.

The red glow disappeared. It only took minutes to be directed to Paul Granger's room as people recognized who they were. Stern-faced security forces stood five-deep around it, but the three of them were passed through without question.

"We're taking him off your hands," Lon assured them as Jae and Lina directed those in the room to leave.

To Lina's eyes, Granger didn't look good to go. He was swollen, almost unrecognizable, his skin purples and blacks and greens. The whites of his eyes were red. A couple fistfuls of red hair were missing from his head. His bed was surrounded with IV drips and monitors.

Good. Lina hoped he hurt all over. Badly.

He sat there, a plastic cup of ice chips halfway to his mouth. As he looked up he dropped it, sending a cascade of shards across his blankets.

"Judgement Day," Londo announced as they grouped themselves around the bed. "Neutrino, this is the ex-Galactic Guard of Earth. We are deporting him."

Granger could actually look worse, for he did so now. He couldn't miss the sheer hatred in their eyes.

"We are summoned," Lina repeated for his sake. "Ruby, please give me a landing picture." She touched her earring. "Wiley, start your telemetry measurements now."

The scene appeared in her mind with alacrity, coming sharply into focus without concentration.

They ported.

Wiley had asked her numerous times how long it would take to do a really long port. What were her limits?

The Galactic Sentinels lived in the center of the Milky Way near the mammoth black hole there, from which they generated the energy their Brigade utilized. Either Wiley or Jae had told her that that was 8,000 parsecs away, which worked out to about 26,000 light years. She'd never ported remotely that far. But this seemed the same as always: constructing the new image so that piece of space, in essence, assembled itself around them, replacing the space they were in. Two minutes for equalizing pressure and electrical potential, asking this new world of Aum what it would willingly take so that no contagion traveled with them…

They were there.

Had it really only taken two minutes or did it just seem like it? Lina had that five-minute time limit for biofiltering. They hadn't dissolved, so maybe it was the same as usual.

It was Jae who took the cautious first step, then a second, more confident one. They were in a mammoth cave. He turned to make sure the others were there, to watch a glove of living rock rise up to envelop Granger and then retreat back into the ground with him as he shrieked.

Light rippled around the center of the cave as if it were under technicolor water with bright sunlight above.

"Radiation?" Jae asked Lon quietly.

Lon checked a readout from his Legion ring. "We're fine."

It was all hewn from dark rock, clearly of geometric design but with many rough surfaces remaining. At a distance in front of them, fully within the brightness, stood a group… of giant tortoises. Under the undulating light they seemed to be deep jewel tones on top and darkest shadows on the bottom. Their shells held lively, intricate geometric patterns.

But really. Turtles. Lina marveled but still shivered at the idea of the actual *Galactic Sentinels*. They were in charge of the Brigade. They'd been around since forever, as far as she was concerned. Maybe millions of years. Each of them. Their Brigade watched over the galaxy, all sixty kazillion star systems.

That Brigade was thus stretched thin. No wonder things could fall through the cracks. But still… Granger. He'd been a colossal mistake, something that should never have happened no matter the size of the cracks.

Jae's staff of authority appeared. He thumped it three times upon the ground. It commanded attention. The three walked forward into the light and Lina could feel… something happening.

**We want to make an impression,** Earth laughed in her mind.

Lina resisted the urge to look at her husbands out of the corners of her eyes, but Wiley's records later revealed that as they walked their appearances morphed in ever-changing aspect. Their costumes changed, became skin tunics and cloaks of fur, then wool, then linen; animal teeth and shark skins, feathers, crystal... Jewelry of bone and crystal. A wind blew their garments around them, and it carried the natural sounds of Earth with it: birds, insects and land animals, whale song, volcanoes, the tides. At times their skin was marked with blue designs all over, but their Three Worlds tattoos constantly glowed golden, even hers from beneath her clothes.

The garments updated, reflecting ages of change and cultures until they were modern day. Then the three stood in their costumes in front of the turtles. Lina was very glad she'd chosen to wear that green outfit to the press conference.

Bright light surrounded them and highlighted faint, ghostly silhouettes of birds and trees and animals around them. Earth whispered to her that humans knew how to put a good ritual together, and had inspired her. Lina laughed softly as she silently relayed that information to her partners. The world was amused, as was this one… Aum.

"I am Jaeson Rallene Starhart, and I am Minister for Earth."

"I am Londo Rand Starhart, and I am Protector of Earth."

"I am Carolina O'Kelly Starhart, and I am Speaker for Earth. She speaks."

She felt the spirit of the Earth begin to possess her and welcomed it. Now that entity spoke through her:

"The Galactic Ruby Guard Brigade is honored throughout the galaxy for its works, and it has been this way for untold millennia. I remember well the many times its members have come to my aid and the aid of my sisters... and those who live upon us.

"But this Guard we bring you today has served dishonorably. For some years he has been misusing the power you have provided him with to cause misery to my children, destruction to me. And now he has dared to try to harm one of my Chosen. All to satisfy his personal lust for even more power. None of this is acceptable. He is banished from my realm. Return to me in your next lifetime, Granger formerly of Earth, and I will be pleased to teach you the harsh lessons you need. But do not return in this lifetime. I cannot easily forgive such misuse of power.

"This does not mean that I will not welcome another Guard to me. But I urge the Sentinels to reexamine their priorities, the qualifications they require of their brigade members. Remember the beginnings, when your ideals were so high and sang across the scope of the galactic threads…"

Lina/Earth began to sing of ancient bravery and courage in the face of trouble that permeated the universe. The song shared hopes of helping others and an organization that reflected the brotherhood that they all desired to demonstrate to the near-infinite worlds of the galaxy. These were the dreams of the Sentinels millennia ago.

Somewhere in a distant corner of her mind, Lina noticed that the song was sung in ancient Aumian, older than the suns back home in the galaxy's arms.

Jae and Lon sang along, weaving their sweet melodies through hers, and the music of Earth permeated the three of them and filled the auditorium. The song came to a triumphant end.

The Earth paused and spoke again. "Send us a hero of old from your ranks, Sentinels, if you can find one, and they will be welcome in my realm and honored for their deeds and heart.

"The same welcome awaits one on my sister world of Aldierra. She is in dire need of help these days."

A powerful voice came out of the rippling darkness. None of the turtles had moved to indicate who spoke. "And what of Sarastor?"

*The Sentinels have heard of us,* Lina thought in awe. *They know of the Three Worlds!*

It was Earth who spoke through her, with a little smile in her words. "Sarastor has the Legion residing on it, Sentinel. Heroes in the old tradition with great power in their hands also. There is no need for a special Guardian there, but Sarastor appreciates the thought.

"So I repeat to the Sentinels of our galaxy: this human is no longer welcome on Earth. He is banished. Thus speaks Gaia." And the spirit of Earth was gone. Lina took a deep breath and shook her head to clear it completely, trying to keep her composure in front of the Sentinels.

There was silence for a beat. Then a voice – was it the same one? For some reason Lina thought not, although it sounded almost the same – announced: "This human will be held pending trial. His membership in the Brigade is suspended, pending a final decision. His Ruby is confiscated for evidence."

Lina reached into her neckline to remove the Ruby, but paused with it between her palms. "This Ruby is innocent," she declared. "This is me talking, not Earth. The Ruby was cruelly used by Granger. It has suffered. It rebelled against him during a crisis, and I am alive because of its actions. So it is a great hero of our world. It is brave and of good heart. Can you offer it safety? Therapy? It needs to recover in a peaceful place."

"If not," Londo crossed his arms across his chest, "it should remain with us. We will keep it safe."

"We will not use it for our own profit," Jae added.

The turtles remained where they were, staring at them. Behind the group the cavern background slowly widened into a much larger one. There, level upon level of Sentinels, made small by distance, watched them as well.

The Sentinels began to hum.

They did it softly, but so many of them created a vibration that began to shake Lina's bones. To get her mind off that, she listened to the melody, for there was a melody in there, plus harmony with only a few discordant notes here and there.

**They're speaking to one another,** Jae surmised. **It's a communal discussion.**

**But everyone's speaking at once.**

**Yes.**

Lina wondered what the Worlds thought of it all and then realized that the thought occurred to her because she could feel them discussing this among themselves, all four of them, including Feith. Without thinking, she began to hum along.

**Lina. Stop. Don't interfere.**

But she let herself go, feeling the energy passing through her from thousands of parsecs away and yet this place as well. Her tune did not quite fit with that of the Sentinels.

It ended long before theirs did.

When the humming stopped, the far chamber closed up again. Three Sentinels made their way out of the near group, sliding like they were on a moving track instead of moving their legs.

They spoke in unison. "We have seen the evidence. Reached a verdict. Paul Granger is expelled from the Galactic Guard Brigade. He will be imprisoned at our Place of Transformation."

"That fast?" Londo asked.

"Transformation?" Jae asked.

"Its name is Exetis."

Jae nodded slowly. **Not going to ask what the escape rate is,** he told his spouses.

"He will be held there until there is no more need."

Lina wasn't sure what that meant, but Jae nodded so she and Londo did as well.

"In the meantime, we will do what we can physically to repair the damage Granger has wrought. Tell Earth not to be concerned when she sees one or more of our troops. For reasons we will not explain, our attention in the recent past has been… inadequate. We will correct that. We have new ways of overseeing all things in the galaxy, including our own people. Very few are undeserving of their place with us. We will root out those who are not, and see to their transformations as well."

"Oh," Lina said. "Thank you. If the rest of the galaxy knew this, they'd thank you as well. Everyone looks to the Galactic Guards for help and inspiration."

"My people had great admiration for the Brigade," Jae added.

"We thank you as well for bringing this to our attention," the Sentinels said. "In the future, if such a situation should occur, do not be so slow in doing so."

"I think this was because people don't want to bother you unnecessarily," Lon put in. "They wanted to be sure of what was going on first. They had to look past the reputation of the Brigade to see the truth."

All three Sentinels tilted their heads to the left and half-closed their eyes. Then they resumed their normal postures. "If you could stand closely together now," they said. "Please."

Lina couldn't hear if her husbands also sucked in a breath, not knowing what was coming next, but she did as commanded.

"Closer. Touch. This should not hurt. Much."

With that, a point just under and behind her right ear stung like the very devil.

"Ouch," Lon complained as he clapped his hand to the same spot.

"This is our thanks to you," the Sentinel explained as the pain went away. "May it serve you well."

"Uh, thank you," Jae said. "Thank you for seeing us."

"And for taking care of Granger. I'd have hated to have to kill him," Lon said. "Without a proper trial, that is."

"Thank you for taking care of the Ruby," Lina said as she handed it into the raised, expectant paw of one of the Sentinels. "Goodbye, Ruby. Feel better. If you need me, just give a call and I'll try my best to find you."

"It will heal," the Sentinel told her and hummed to the Ruby.

It hummed back, a happy note.

# 20

They arrived in Starhaven's living room, four bags of luggage, two Legion duffels, a stack of stasi-keeps with hot food Londo had thought worth hoarding, and a large box of Jae's souvenirs from the tour, all gathered around them.

It was deep dusk through the wall of south-facing windows. A glimmer far down in the distance was all to be seen of the lake set in the Wyoming mountain valley. Ribbons of high clouds caught the last of the sunset.

Lina ran both hands down her face. It had been a long day even though it was still late morning if you went by her time via the Tour. These days she seemed to pack a lot more than normal into her waking hours.

She could hear a TV in the, what was it, west? wing, but there were towering piles of building materials between them and it. Young voices chattered back and forth over what sounded like a commercial. There was a squeal of delight. That was good. These must be the White Puma's great grandkids. "Grandkits," as the famed ParaNet hero called them.

"I'll take the luggage upstairs," Lon told them. He piled it all up and flew off two stories above them to deposit in the master bedroom.

The food should go in the kitchen. At least it wouldn't need refrigeration, which was good, as the pathetic fridge there wasn't large enough to take the boxes. These were meals she didn't remember or had never gotten to, that Lon wanted her to try because he thought she'd like them. There were some for Jae as well, who'd been relegated to Legion combat meals for much of the Tour duty and was overdue some good food. As Lina reached down to gather them, Jae intercepted. He hefted them as easily as Lon might, since he used the antigrav systems of his Legion Array to make them lighter, and trotted off to the kitchen.

"Thanks."

That left Lina with… What? Now that she was home her mind was going bless-edly blank. But she needed to see her cats before she caught some rest. She whistled the pattern she'd always used to call her herd for supper. They all felt like they'd been fed, though.

The voices stopped. Then came the clacking sound of claws on concrete. Bran's unique, "Where are you, Mama?" meow.

"Babies!" Lina called. "Babies!" Oh, her marvelous, wonderful cats!

Here came the entire pack galloping toward her, even ancient Fafhrd. She knelt and held out her arms. "My babies!"

Moosie got to her first, arcing through the air in a mighty leap that landed him hard on her left shoulder. The others were only seconds behind him. Lina sprawled to a sitting position on the floor, gathering them in, cooing to them, trying to pet them all at once.

"I'm so sorry we left for so long. It couldn't be helped. Sweetie, sweetie! Hello! Hello! I love you. Babies!" She laughed as they piled on, each seeking the hugs they were due.

Lon and Jae returned to watch the reunion. Molly spared Londo a juicy hiss when he reached for the box of souvenirs.

The grandkits, two girls and a boy, all young teens, stood back, but Jae waved them near. He and his spouses thanked them for taking care of the herd and asked about any problems. The kits had pictures to show them, and Lon and Jae laughed at them while Lina tried to see around her furbabies, who pawed at her if she ne-glected rubs. Both the girls gaped at beautiful Jae as if they'd been struck by Cupid's arrow. After Lina was assured that the kits would email the photos, she returned full attention to her charges.

Fafhrd took Lina's lap and was joined by Obi. Ember stretched across Lina's right leg, even ignoring Jae, to whom she'd taken a fancy when he'd visited Earth before. Moosie stayed a few minutes lying on his back in Lina's arms like an infant, purring as loud as only he could with his extra-large nose as she scratched his chest, but eventually he got down to sort out who these strange men were. Molly took his place and kneaded biscuits against Lina's shoulder.

Bran persisted in clinging to Lina's left leg, unwilling to let go. Katie lay on her back, a trust pose she rarely took, and let Lina scratch her chin, though not her belly. After a while she straightened and came over to sit next to Lina's side.

"This is excellent," Lina declared. "We're all home. I'm back with the cats. There are no cameras, no press. No terrorists or explosions or torture." She took a deep breath and then let it out. "No strangers. Well…" She glanced at the kits, grimaced and shrugged an apology.

"You'll get to know us, ma'am," the boy in the group said. "We go to all the ParaNet parties."

"Oh, good," Lina said faintly. "Parties. 'Ma'am.' I feel old." She took another cleansing breath. "I don't want to be rude, but could y'all let me have some time here? Alone? Just me and the cats. This has all been… a bit much." She looked at her husbands. "Give me fifteen, twenty minutes. Please."

"Sure thing."

Lon walked the kits to their rooms and their supplies there with Jae in tow, chatting to one of the enamored girls. As they packed, Lon transferred catsitting payments into their accounts with Jae watching the process with interest.

"We may be needing your services now and then," Lon told them as they boggled at their wages. "Would you be interested?"

Would they! And definitely if those services would be needed during ski season, by which time the house would be in much better shape than it was… or so Lon claimed.

Jae looked around at the outlines of rooms, of walls still barely carved out of the mountainside. How quick was Terran engineering? In the recording where Londo had met Lina's parents, Lina had muttered something about how at least two years would be needed to complete construction. Jae scratched his stomach and considered the situation as ParaNet transporters sparkled the kits home, wherever that was.

Lon's phone rang and he fished it out of his vest. "*Allo,* Hal."

Jae bent his head to hear the other side of the conversation, though he couldn't hear much.

"No, not today," Lon said as he checked his watch. "We just now got in. I figure twelve or eighteen hours to decompress," he announced. "That seems like it's going to mean sleep as hard as we can. Then we've got to pack again before we head off to Aldierra. We want to check on Sunstorm, Dinah and Mart – and Demi too; we're running up too many casualties – on Sarastor en route." He shrugged at no one in the room. "*Aucune idée.* We'll see what we run into. I'll be in touch."

Jae heard a sentence that included "grandkids" from the phone's speaker.

Londo let out a laugh. "We are so not ready for those right now. Or in the near future." He listened for a few more moments. "Yes, we've talked about it. But not now. Not for the next year at least. We've got to get things started." The response took more than a few moments, but it still made Lon smile. "*Bon.* You do that." And then he cut the call.

"Grandkids?" Jae asked.

"Not working on them today. You?"

Jae let out a short snort. "Not me. I like that sleep idea you had, as long as it's followed by something more interesting. Is yours itching?" He scratched the place behind his ear where the Sentinels had done whatever they'd done.

"Not anymore. I take it all that means is that they've figured out the touch effect with us."

"It would seem. Nothing to do about it. We'll have Wiley check us out sometime this next week, see if he can figure what they did. In the meantime, I should start my kol-vanaschen to pack," Jae said, and spoke into his Legion ring, to the equipment in his Legion apartment on Sarastor. "This will take more supplies than the Tour. We're going to be living there, right?"

"Andri wants us quartered at HQ."

"Andri doesn't have a say in Three Worlds."

"I want us here."

Jae shook his head. "I have a feeling that Lina might be too tired some days to port us. I want us to keep together as much as possible, on the same planet at the least. Aldierra's a dangerous place. Worse now since the Ultimatum's been put into effect. Lina's not used to trouble."

Lon rubbed his nose to think. "I'll check how our transporter system is progressing. We'll have the system up within the next couple days."

"Good."

Lon looked around at his beloved, nascent Starhaven as they strolled back to join Lina. Its blueprints required major revisions already. He should hire an independent engineer to make sure he'd gotten them right. Kurt would have to put together a good-sized construction crew. They would need transportation from… wherever they decided to use as a base here in Wyoming. He'd have to check out equipment to build a subterranean system, one large enough to handle serious freight.

Work on top of work on top of work. As Papa Mike said, "That's why they pay you the big bucks."

"I'll call Kurt before we leave. Maybe we can have Starhaven finished by the time we're through seeing Aldierra through this."

"I know you arranged rooms for our first nights on Aldierra, but we'll need a permanent place there as well," Jae said in a low voice. "It should be a headquarters, like Starhaven will be; a home that can handle extras. The highest security."

Jae's first home and all its people had been destroyed when he was a boy. The Legion had given him a home, but the Legion was duty; the "home" it offered came with restrictions and obligations. Londo nodded. Home and Jae were important. "We'll get that. It might be a week or so in the hotel, though."

They both came to a stop. Lina had fallen asleep on the cement floor. The cats made a blanket around and on top of her, sleeping as well except for ancient Fafhrd, who slowly blinked at them.

Jae crouched down to make sure Lina was breathing. "We've broken her."

"Don't even joke about that," Lon said quickly. "No one gets sick or injured any more. Is that clear?"

"Yes, Lon-Lon." Jae waited a moment before looking up to his husband. "You're the best extrovert around. But Lina and I, we're more introverted. Crowds and strangers sap our energy. We need recovery time. Things will be more chaotic from here."

Londo rubbed his nose.

"I can teach her the tricks I've learned," Jae told him. "Her therapist – and Lon, we need to get her a permanent therapist within the next five days – can teach her as well. Right now these cats are helping to balance her energy. And she theirs, I suppose."

"I was afraid of this. This is why I didn't just ask the kits to stay on. The cats keep Lina sane, or at least that's what she thinks."

Jae made a sound of agreement that turned into one of doubt. "She told Wiley that cats shouldn't be moved around. Bad for their psyches."

"They'll move to Aldierra while we're there. And Sarastor while we're there as well. If we're only gone a few hours, they can stay wherever we started from. Now they're Starharts. They adapt."

"Starharts." Jae rose to his feet. "Aren't we all now."

"For better or for worse, as Terrans say.

"*Voyons.*" Lon began to count the cats to make sure all seven were present. "There's Fat Cat, and Other Fat Cat, Big Nose Cat, and Dead Cat Who's Not Dead Yet Cat, and Hellcat…" Molly's head rose up just long enough for her to let loose a good hiss. "And…"

"You'll have to learn their names. I'll give you three days, but you'll start with mine. Ember." Jae rubbed the ears of the sleeping cat who favored him.

"Three days. Lina made cheat sheets for ParaNet Security and the kits. I'll get a copy for me. *Donc,* Ember is the gray one. Ah, like wood ashes; Ember. Got it." Lon nodded at Lina's sleeping form. "Now. Suggestions as to how we extricate her from this and get her to a bed."

They had to ponder that problem for some time.

## MY THANKS

…to intrepid editor Eugenia Lazarus. We won't talk about Day 4 of the Tour, will we? No no no.

…Also to Radleigh Valentine for his amazing psi classes, as well as Sue B. (these days Sue H.), my original teacher who taught us so much.


## ABOUT THE AUTHOR


When you think of strong women and strange worlds, think Carol A. Strickland.

Although born in a small town in Illinois noted for its Nineteenth Century demonic possession cases, Carol claims that all those voices inside her head are a result of having stories to tell and books to write. Even so, her strange devotion to and study of Wonder Woman would seem to indicate an abby-normal brain.

A one-time comics letterhack and outspoken member of various comics message boards, Carol has found herself the basis for two comic book villains (at times her opinions have not been taken well by the books' creators) (both villains were soundly thrashed) (and both, for some perverse reason, were male) and had one superhero wear her costume design. (Light Lass!)

Carol has also become an award-winning painter and certified tarot reader. Her primary talent, though, is procrastination. See what else she wastes time on at her website: www.CarolAStrickland.com or check out her other books at www.CarolAStricklandBooks.com

www.ingramcontent.com/pod-product-compliance
Lightning Source LLC
Chambersburg PA
CBHW071012180726
48291CB00004B/1429